BUCK HILL FALLS

BUCK HILL FALLS

ONE SUMMER LASTS FOREVER

NED HENTZ

iUniverse®

BUCK HILL FALLS
ONE SUMMER LASTS FOREVER

iUniverse books may be ordered through booksellers or by contacting:

iUniverse
1663 Liberty Drive
Bloomington, IN 47403
www.iuniverse.com
844-349-9409

ISBN: 978-1-6632-2101-8 (sc)
ISBN: 978-1-6632-2102-5 (e)

Print information available on the last page.

iUniverse rev. date: 06/02/2021

DEDICATION

This book is dedicated to my beautiful wife Kate who never runs out of patience, love and compassion for our family and friends and is finally dreaming in Italian.

Special thanks to MC Hentz, the talented singer/songwriter and screenwriter based in Los Angeles who introduced me to *Save the Cat* by Blake Snyder and helped provide some crucial insights. I also want to thank my wonderful sister Carrie, who shared one special summer with me at *Buck Hill Falls* and who makes the world a better place every day for people less fortunate than ourselves. Her quote from *Uncle John's Band* by the *Grateful Dead* in our high school yearbook says it best. *"Ain't no time to hate, barely time to wait. Oh-oh, what I want to know, where does the time go?"*

BUCK HILL FALLS

WINTER LINGERED LONGER than usual during the second half of my senior year in high school in the early 1980's, or maybe it just seemed that way. My friends and I were ready to graduate, even though most of us had no idea what was going to happen next. The only thing any of us knew for sure was that we were finished with high school. Some of my friends were going to college. A few had jobs lined up. Several were about to enlist in the Army.

The world was a completely different place then. Honestly, you wouldn't recognize it. The only people with cell phones were members of the *Star Ship Enterprise*. We talked to each other in person. If that wasn't possible, there seemed to be a pay phone on every corner. The internet hadn't been invented yet, although the *National Science Foundation* had started to fund national supercomputer centers at several universities across the United States.

There were long periods of time where absolutely nothing happened. An actor had taken over the presidency from a peanut farmer from Georgia. *Eye of the Tiger* was the number one song on the billboard top 100 followed by *Don't you want me baby* by *The Human League. Hall and Oats* were popular too. Not so much with me, but I did go to one of their concerts at the Allentown Fairgrounds in Pennsylvania, not far from where I grew up, with a girl named Veronica who I fell in love with that summer and still think about from time to time.

While I was asleep in my childhood bedroom, a dark maroon '66 Ford Galaxie ragtop with one cockeyed headlight, drove past the rusting blast furnaces and smoke stacks of what was once one of the largest steel producing and shipbuilding companies in the world. Years before the first shots were fired in the Civil War, *The Bethlehem Rolling Mill and Iron Company* produced rails for the rapidly expanding network of railroads and eventually produced heavy guns and armor plating for the US Navy. After belching clouds of black soot into the sky above the rooftops of houses and schools and businesses in the

Lehigh valley for nearly 150 years, Bethlehem Steel filed for bankruptcy. As manufacturing jobs moved overseas, groups of eager developers, armed with generous tax incentives, worked hard to turn the former steel mill into a hotel and casino only to find themselves unable to move forward due to a worldwide shortage of structural steel.

As the Galaxie ragtop rolled up and down the deserted streets of my home town, Floyd "The Hitman" Hardapple, a former middleweight boxing champion, reached down into a sea of neatly rolled newspapers and tossed them one at a time out his open window onto the gravely driveways and weedy lawns of the neglected houses in my neighborhood. On the floor next to him was an unregistered *Sig Sauer* handgun with the safety off, because you never knew who might be roaming around the streets in the early hours of the morning. The bold headline that day announced, "*Stocks drop as layoffs continue*" while a monotone voice on the AM radio station in the car confirmed the depressing news.

"*Wall Street is expected to continue its downward spiral today as overseas markets opened lower than anticipated. Up next, weather from your local meteorologist. Good morning*

Pennsylvania! Stormy Waters here with today's forecast for the Lehigh Valley and vicinity. Don't forget your umbrella on the way to work this morning. A cold front is rolling down from Canada and going to hook up with warm air from the Carolinas resulting heavy rain and thunderstorms in the early afternoon stopping sometime around rush hour. And speaking of the commute, back in sixty seconds with your traffic update brought to you by the friendly bakers at Tastykake."

My mother, an attractive woman in her early forties, had gotten up early that morning before going to work as a receptionist at a home heating oil company. She didn't love her job, but she didn't hate it either. It was steady and enabled her to pay our bills and put food on the table for the two of us and a large stray cat that had wandered into our kitchen several years ago. We named him Waldo, after one of my favorite characters in a popular children's book.

It's a long story, and we'll get into it later, but my father disappeared shortly after I was born and my mother had been dating this guy named Dwight who, in my opinion, was only one evolutionary stage away from being a Neanderthal. Every time they went on a date, I longed for her to come home and tell me they broke up. I had no idea what she saw in him, other than the fact that he was single, had a job and as far as she knew, had never spent time in prison.

Before she left the house that morning, she called upstairs to tell me she wouldn't be home for dinner because she was going on a date with Dwight. Somewhere in my slumbering teenage brain, what she said registered. As she was about to dash out the door she checked her watch and then looked up at the clock on our kitchen wall and noticed there was a 20 minute time difference. Shaking her wrist she muttered, *"Can't you two ever get along?!"* Realizing she was late, she grabbed her car keys off a hook on the kitchen wall and left the coffee mug she had just poured for herself sitting on the breakfast table.

When I finally woke up, more than five hours later, my alarm clock told me it was 11:25. Wondering why it didn't go off at 7:15, like it was supposed to, I realized I'd probably forgotten to set it. I'd been forgetting a lot of things lately. Now that school was over, and graduation was only a few days away, the routine that I had been following for my entire life had ended. Other than my job stocking shelves at *Hardware Depot,* there was no reason to get up in the morning. It was "Senior Week" at my high school when we had the whole place to ourselves to hang out with our friends, use the weight room or shoot baskets in the empty gymnasium. The only thing left for me to do was clean out my locker and drop off a few books at the library.

My small upstairs bedroom was cluttered with the usual teenage stuff. A *Star Wars* poster and a picture of Phoebe Cates coming out of the pool from the movie *Fast Times at Ridgemont High*. On the dresser next to my bed was a record player and my favorite album, *Night Moves* by Bob Seger. Hanging from a hook on my bedroom door was my apron from *Hardware Depot* with my nametag that said *"Daniel Barnes, Trainee"*. A half-eaten bag of *Bugles* was on the floor next to my bed. After I showered and brushed my teeth, I clomped down the stairs in my untied hiking boots and poured myself a bowl my favorite cereal, *Cap'n Crunch*.

The house was so still and quiet the only sound I heard was the ticking of the clock on the wall and the *"crunch, crunch, crunch"* of the cereal inside my mouth. A calendar on our refrigerator reminded me this was *"Senior Week"* and my eighteenth birthday was a few days away. My mother had drawn a smiling stick figure character of me on the calendar wearing a top hat adorned with flaming candles and the number 18 printed in large numerals on my tee shirt. Happy, *"Stick Figure Danny"* presented a stark contrast to the sad and lonely teenager sitting in an empty house that day eating breakfast cereal at noon.

Checking my Casio digital watch I saw it was 1:23 and decided to inflate the tires on my Schwinn Varsity bicycle and peddle the 5 miles of sidewalk to my high school and clean out my locker. The place was pretty much deserted when I got there except for a janitor riding up and down the long hallway on a sit down floor scrubber trying to remove a year's worth of scuff marks.

When I was just about finished emptying out my locker, I noticed my favorite English teacher, Mr. Ezra, leaving his classroom with an armful of books. I always liked Mr. Ezra. He was one of the only black teachers in our high school and he was always impeccably dressed. Even that day, when our school was out of session, he was wearing a dark suit and tie with a neatly folded handkerchief stuffed in his coat pocket. For some reason, Mr. Ezra had taken an interest in me and encouraged me to apply to several competitive colleges even though my guidance counselor, and most of the people I knew, felt they were well beyond my reach. On top of that, even if I managed to get accepted at one of those schools, my mom and I still hadn't figured out how we were going to pay the tuition.

When Mr. Ezra got to my locker he shifted his stack of books to one side and reached out his hand. *"Congratulations Danny. I'm going to miss seeing you sitting in the third row."*

After I thanked him for introducing me to Harper Lee and *To kill a Mockingbird* and his favorite book, *Stop time* by Frank Conroy, he asked what my plans were for the summer.

"Really nothing much" I told him. *"I'm still working afternoons at Hardware Depot. My mom needs me to take her to the clinic twice a week for her treatments. They really tire her out and she can't drive home afterwards. But they seem to be working. Other than that, not much."*

Looking to change the subject, he asked *"Well, you must be excited about college. You should be proud of yourself. Not many of your fellow classmates got into universities as good as William & Mary. I'm not blowing smoke because I went there. You're going to love Virginia."*

"I hope so," I told him. *"I can't thank you enough for your recommendations. They must have really helped. Otherwise I'm pretty sure I would never have gotten in."*

"Nonsense," he said. *"You worked hard. And you got in on your own merits. I had nothing to do with it. Believe me, they are fully aware that the salary of a high school English teacher isn't going to do a damn thing for their endowment. All I did was put in a good word."*

As I pulled the tape off a picture of my mom that had been in my locker for the last three and a half years, I mentioned that her boyfriend had offered to help me get a job at the particle board factory where he worked to earn some money to help pay my tuition.

"That'll help." he said. *"But don't forget about those scholarships I told you about. They are out there. You just have to go after them. Don't be passive, Danny. You have to stand up for yourself. Too many people are passive these days. Waiting around for things to come to them. That's not the way the world works. You have to stand up for what you believe. Listen, I don't usually give my students advice, because they rarely listen, but just this once, I'm going to make an exception. I've watched hundreds of*

students, maybe even thousands, pass through these hallways. Some of them smarter and more gifted than yourself. But success isn't always about being smart or talented. It's often about persistence and determination. What's most important is that you find something you love. Whatever that thing is, work really hard until you master it. It might take a long time. Sometimes years. But that's okay. Believe in yourself and don't ever give up. Nine times out of ten, we are our own worst enemies."

The next time I saw Mr. Ezra was at graduation where he sat patiently listening to our principal praise the parents and the teachers for their hard work raising and educating us and then went on to recite a series of statements that seem to have been plagiarized from a self-help book and, from the reaction of the audience, didn't resonate with anyone but himself. Finally, after thirty seven and a half minutes, he left us with a quote from Mark Twain.

"Twenty years from now you will be more disappointed by the things you didn't do than by the ones you did do. So throw off the bowlines. Sail away from the safe harbor. Catch the trade winds in your sails. Explore. Dream. Discover."

After graduation, a few of us decided to hike up to the stone quarry behind the high school and wash off the pomp and circumstance. It was technically off limits, and we would have been called into the principal's office if the school found out, but now that we had graduated there wasn't much they could do. It was an unusually hot day considering it was the middle of May and beneath our silk caps and gowns we were drenched with sweat.

Nobody said a word as we walked along the rusting railroad tracks past the abandoned boiler factory on the way to the quarry. Will, who was president of the robotics team and the quietest member of our group finally commented on how lame he thought the graduation ceremony was. *"They're all lame"* said Doug who towered over him and the rest of us at 6'6".

"High school is just a way to keep us out of the job market, so our parents can make enough money to retire. Then, they realized they needed more time, so they invented college. If my parents would have let me, I would have skipped high school and joined the army.

"That's not the way it works Doug" said Will. *"Schools were created to help people overcome poverty, and ignorance. But I guess in your case, they failed miserably."*

Not acknowledging Will's put down, Doug reached down between the railroad tracks, picked up a rock and threw it through one of the last remaining windows of the boiler factory.

"Nice toss!" said Tony who had played football with Doug and was a talented musician.

"*Yup, I still got it.*" Doug said confidently.

When we came to a junction in the tracks, we followed a spur that took us to a stone quarry filled with water and surrounded by high cliffs. Standing at the edge of the tallest cliff, I shouted *"Hello!"* and a few seconds later I heard myself answering, *"Hello!"* Immediately, Will and Doug begin hooting and hollering until the quarry was filled with the sounds of our voices bouncing off the stone walls. After the novelty of hearing our voices wore off, we stripped off our clothes down to our underwear and jumped off the rock ledge into the cold water of the quarry and hung out in the sun on the warm rocks.

Looking at the clouds above our heads we talked about whatever came into our minds. Doug said he was going to enlist in the army and become a military policeman. Because of his height he was an imposing figure, even without a uniform and a gun. Will was fascinated by robots and was trying to build one in his basement. He had named it PAM, which stood for *Personal Animatronic Machine.* Whenever we asked him how Pam was doing, people thought we were talking about his girlfriend, which in a way we were. If you wanted to know about the three laws of robotics according to Isaac Asimov, Will would be happy to elaborate.

As president of the Robotics Club Will had led our high school to the finals in Orlando, Florida where he had been offered a job right out of high school working for the Department of Defense. The catch, he soon found out, was he would be developing weapons for the military. Instead, he accepted a full scholarship at Virginia Tech and was looking forward to pursuing his passion there in the fall. His roommate would have to get used to living with Pam.

Tony Bagnoli had shoulder length brown hair and was the most handsome member of our group. His parents were both Italian and he had a dark complexion and always looked like he was in need of a shave. When we were in high school they were in the middle of an ugly divorce and when the arguments eventually became violent, Tony moved in with his girlfriend Phoebe. She was several years older than us and had gone to art school somewhere in New England. After a really cold winter, and the infamous snowstorm of 1978, she decided to come home and pursue a career as a singer. For a while she worked as a waitress at *Chili's* until she saved enough money to be able to afford a small apartment in an up an coming part of town. On Saturday mornings she sang with a band that Tony had put together. After he helped her move out of her parent's house and into the apartment she had rented he never left.

When I asked Tony how things were going with the band he said. *"We're going on tour as soon as we can find a manager we can trust. Not as easy as you might think. Hey, I trust you Danny. Why don't you manage the band? Phoebe likes you. And I know the only reason you hang around me is because you have a crush on her. I have eyes, brother. I see what you're up to. Waiting for us to have an argument, so you can pick up the pieces and finally get what you've been dreaming about for so long."*

Tony had what people call 'street smarts'. Not that he didn't do well in high school. Tony did well at things Tony was interested in. He wasn't wrong. I had a crush on Phoebe. To be honest, there wasn't much not to like about Phoebe. She was attractive, intelligent, talented and several years older. Girls like that never fell for guys like me. The best I could hope for was for her to treat me like a younger brother, but I played along, just to piss him off.

"Congratulations Tony! You figured it out. I never really liked you, just her. But when we get married, we're going to need a band and I'm going to need a best man. So it makes sense."

After we fist bumped, Tony told me he was thinking about changing his name to *"T Bone"*. *"Not many rock stars named Tony,"* he said. When I mentioned Tony Bennett, he shot me a look. *"Okay, you're fired. Tony Bennett is not a rock star. Maybe to my Nonna, but not to anyone our age. That's not even his real name. The man to whom you are referring, Anthony Dominick Benedetto, changed his name when he was my age. So there. Who would you rather see in concert? Tony Bagnoli or T Bone Bagnoli?"*

He had a point. But it would take a long time for me to get used to calling him 'T-Bone'.

I woke up with a sick feeling in my stomach on the morning of my birthday. It was a Tuesday, and my mother had already gone to work, but she left a card on the breakfast table wishing me a happy birthday and telling me she loved me. We planned to go to Chili's that night to celebrate, but I had forgotten to ask my friends, so it was probably just going to be just me and my mom and possibly, unfortunately, Dwight. The drinking age in Pennsylvania had been raised to 21, but across the river in New Jersey there were still some places where it was 18. A few of my friends had promised to take me to Burlington that weekend so we could go to the Brickwall Tavern where I could buy my first beer without having to show a fake ID.

As I sat there on the couch that morning, watching a talk show on television, I heard the mailman coming up the steps to the front porch, which was unusual because he always left the mail in the mailbox at the foot of our driveway. After he knocked loudly three times on the warped screen door I got up off the couch to see what he wanted. Opening the front door a crack I meekly said, "Yes?"

"Certified letter for Daniel Patrick Barnes" he said without looking up from the stack of letters he was holding in his one

gloved hand. *"It's going to require a signature. Is Mr. Barnes at home? I'll need some form of identification if he's he is willing and able to sign."*

I had never received a certified letter before and I wasn't sure what to do. When the mailman seemed to become impatient, I took out my license and showed him and signed the green card that was on the front of the letter. After he examined my license and compared the signatures he said *"Happy birthday Mr. Barnes."* and pushed the letter through the crack in the door. Not sure if I should open it, I left it sitting on the breakfast table, next to my birthday card, and went back to watching television before my shift started at the Hardware Depot.

Before we went to Chili's that night, my mom poured herself a glass of red wine and we opened the letter together while we sat on the couch in the living room. It was from an attorney named Bob Robertson who worked at a Philadelphia Law firm and claimed to have been a close friend of my father. His name had never come up, but I could tell by the look on my mother's face that she must have known him. The letter stated that he had some important information about my father that he needed to discuss with me privately now that I was 18. It was fine for me to share the conversation with my mother, but he wanted to discuss it with me personally beforehand. At the bottom of the letter, in elegant penmanship, he'd written:

"Can we meet tomorrow morning for breakfast at the Tick Tock Diner? I happen to be passing through your neck of the woods. It would be nice to meet you in person."

When I asked my mother who Bob Robertson was and why he might be reaching out, she didn't seem to want to talk about it. *"Bob was someone who was a friend of your fathers, and mine I suppose. Although we never had the chance to get to know each other. He was supposed to tell me what happened to your father, where he went, but I always got the feeling he was hiding something. The last time we spoke we had a terrible argument. I said some things I maybe shouldn't have said. But I was frustrated and angry. And I never heard from him again. Until now. You may as well meet with him. Have breakfast. See what he has to say."*

The following morning, at the *Tick Tock Diner*, I saw a man sitting by himself in a booth across from a rough-looking group of long-haul truckers. He was about fifty years old, very tan considering it was still Spring, and confident enough to be wearing a canary yellow polo shirt, a white belt and lime green golf pants. Where I came from, people didn't dress that way. When he saw me standing in the entrance to the diner he stood up and waved me over to his booth.

"Danny boy" he said as he handed me a menu and gestured for me to take a seat. *"No need to ask if it's really you. You are the spitting image of your father. I feel like I'm seeing a ghost. Thanks for coming. I assume you've been here before, being so close to where you live."*

When I said I had never been there, he told me his theory about why diners have the best food. *"They only offer the basics."* he said. *"Good, honest, American food. Burgers, meat loaf, mashed potatoes. And because most diners have galley kitchens, it's easier for cooks to move from one dish to another and for servers to get the meals to the tables more quickly."*

As we ate breakfast, Bob told me he had a place in the Pocono's at Buck Hill Falls which was started as a Quaker community. *"It's a cottage, actually. That's what they call homes there. Not because they are small. Some of them are actually quite large. But we call them cottages. My grandfather built it in 1923. I grew up going there. Eventually, I inherited it."*

"The Poconos" Bob explained, *"Are a hidden gem tucked away in the middle of a pine forest. Lakes, waterfalls, canoeing, if you like that sort of stuff. It's not like the Hamptons, where the only thing people want to talk about is which B-list Hollywood celebrity was seen ordering a Long Island Ice Tea or a Slippery Nipple at Summers Beach and Dance Club in Quogue.*

When we had finished our breakfast, Bob waved the waitress back over to the booth and asked her to please bring the check and top off our two coffees.

"So, on a more serious note son, let me explain why we're here. Your father and I were friends. During our senior year at Princeton we were roommates. Your dad was a wizard with numbers and I have what people call 'the gift of gab'. After we graduated, we needed jobs, so he went into investments and I became a lawyer. Long story short, your father got involved with some people he should have avoided, and under some very unusual circumstances, he disappeared. Rest assured, his disappearance had nothing to do with his love for you and your mother, whom he worshipped and adored. They planned to get married as soon as his divorce was finalized. However when things dragged on, and your mother became pregnant, he asked

me to prepare a will to keep as much money as possible away from his soon to be ex-wife and provide for his future offspring. Your father was what people call a 'self-made man', and his time spent in private equity left behind a strong distaste for people he felt were dishonest or immoral. Even if they turned out to be members of his own family. So after two years of legal wrangling, we attached something called a 'morals clause' to his estate to prevent his soon to be ex-wife, and any future progeny, from inheriting any more of his hard earned money than he felt they deserved. Then we took out an expensive insurance policy on his life."

After the waitress brought him the check he handed her a brand new $100 bill.

"Let's see. Where was I? Morals clause! You probably haven't the foggiest idea what a morals clause is, so let me try to explain. A morals clause is something that is often built into an executive's compensation package to prevent him, or her in some cases, from doing things that could negatively impact a company's reputation or stock price. Hiring a prostitute on a business trip, for example might not go over so well for the CEO of a soap company that claims to be 99% pure and "Trusted for Generations". Charges

of tax evasion or accepting bribes would not be a good look for the CEO of H&R Block or the Chairman of Dun & Bradstreet."

"So I can tell by the look on your face you are probably thinking, what does this have to do with me? I'm not the CEO of anything. At the negotiating table for your father's divorce we had simply run out of options. They were being completely unreasonable. What your father was trying to do was make sure whatever money he had at the time of his passing would be left to a good and deserving person. Someone who would not be corrupted. Unfortunately, he is not around to make that determination. Any questions before I continue?"

When I didn't have any questions, he took a big sip of coffee and continued.

"So here's where things got complicated. Since your father's body was never recovered, there was a chance that he didn't die, that he is, in fact, still living. At least that's the way the insurance company viewed it. There was an investigation and they came up with some evidence that he might have taken up residence in Venezuela and assumed a new identity. I hired some people to look into it, but after six months they weren't able to find a speck of evidence. They were convinced the insurance company had

fraudulently planted evidence so they wouldn't have to pay the premium. Seven years went by and we were still unable to able to settle the claim. Then, there was a series of near bankruptcies and a few leveraged buyouts and the by the time the dust settled, the original issuer had seen seven different corporate headquarters."

"Your mother was convinced that your father ran out on her. On both of you. And that I was covering up for him. She even hired a detective to listen to my phone calls. I told her it was a waste of money. When she didn't find out anything, we had a heated discussion and she hung up on me. I can't blame her for feeling angry. We were all angry. Things hadn't turned out the way we expected. So that's a lot for a young man to process. I'm sorry about that. But I thought you should know. So I've talked for a long time. Why don't you tell me a little about yourself"

After I told Bob about some of my interests and my largely mediocre high school career ending with being accepted at William & Mary, a light seemed to go off in his head. *"Well, from what you've told me I'm sure your father would be very proud of you. I miss him terribly and I sincerely wish you had an opportunity to get to know him as well as I did. Much like yourself, he was a fine young man. You know, as I was sitting here listening to you talk, thinking about your father, an idea popped into my head. From what you've just told me you really don't have a lot going on this summer. Why don't you spend the summer working at Buck Hill, where I happen to have some influence? You could be a camp counselor, or something similar, at the day camp run by the Inn. You'd be perfect. Room and board are free, so you could save everything you earn. I'll be there on weekends, to keep an eye on things, and the two of us could get to know each other. I know that would make your father happy. You'd have to check with your mother, of course. Make sure it's okay with her. I already know what it's like to be on her bad side. Why don't you give it some thought? I'll write down my phone number at the cottage and you can give me a call over the weekend. Whatever you decide, I'm glad you stopped by and we finally had a chance to meet. Be sure to say 'hi' to your mom. Tell her what we talked about and let her know I would love to see her some time. She's a real pistol!"*

After I finished my shift at the Hardware Depot, my mom and I had a quiet dinner and as we were cleaning the dishes, I told her what Bob had said about my father. She'd always been uncomfortable talking about my father and avoided it whenever possible. Since they had not been married when I was born, I was technically what some people might call "illegitimate" or even worse, a bastard. Statistically speaking, children born out of wedlock have the deck of life stacked against them from the day they are born. For children living in single family homes the odds of poverty, low education level, criminality and drug use were great. I had been fortunate. My mother had done everything in her power to bring me up properly. Soon I was going off to college and I felt bad leaving her all alone and now someone from the past who knew my father had asked me to leave home even earlier than we had planned. I told her it was generous of Bob to offer me a job for the summer at his club or resort or whatever it was but there was no way I could possibly accept. Plus, I was looking forward to spending time with my friends.

"This is our last chance to be together" I pleaded. *"Doug's about to enlist in the Army. Tony and Phoebe are preparing for a road trip. I have no idea what Will is up to and you need someone to drive you back and forth to your treatments. There's just too much going on."*

After she thought about what I had just told her she put her hand on my shoulder and said. "*Look, Danny, I hear what you're saying, and I get that you want to be with your friends. You're not wrong. It makes sense. But someone is opening a door for you. And I know from experience, that doors open and they close. I appreciate you wanting to keep me company and drive me to my treatments, but there are volunteers for that. People who enjoy helping people. I'll be fine. I'm a survivor. It's time for you to think about yourself, about what's best for you. You've never been away from home and you're going to college in a few months. This is a chance for you to meet some new people, have some fun. I'll be fine, I promise. The thing that would make me the most happy would be seeing you happy. And your dad would agree.*"

I had trouble getting to sleep that night, thinking about all the things I had learned about my father and wondering if he was in fact still alive and living under an assumed name somewhere in South America. If that was the case, I imagined he would have reached out at some point to his old friend and college roommate, Bob Robertson. But that hadn't happened. I didn't want to leave my friends and my mother, but they would be less than two hours away and we could probably still see each other. The look in her eyes that night told me she had a few regrets about the roads not taken and she didn't want me to make the same mistakes.

The next morning I called Mr. Robertson on the number he had given me but nobody picked up the phone so I left a message on his answering machine thanking him for his offer and telling him that I would accept. I decided not to give my notice at The Hardware Depot or let anyone know I was leaving until I heard back from him, which I did later that night.

"Danny!" he said. *"Got your message and I'm delighted you'll be working at Buck Hill this summer. I'll contact the activities director right away and tell him to find a place for you. His name is Julian Snow and we're lucky to have him. He's an Ivy, like your dad and me. Went to Cornell. Not Princeton or Harvard but an Ivy nonetheless. Graduated third in his class, I'm told. We haven't met, but I hear he's a fine fellow. You can bunk with him. There's a cottage behind the Inn for employees and he's the only one there. So pack up your belongings son. Everything starts on Monday, so if I were you I would get here as soon as possible. Go*

to the Inn and get yourself registered. Then, once you're situated, give me a call."

I felt a little better once the wheels had been put in motion, but I still hadn't told my friends and I was looking forward to getting that over with. On Thursdays we usually went to *Yocco's* for hot dogs, so I called Tony and had him round up the usual suspects and we met on Liberty Street and sat in a booth in the back. I had my usual; two hot dogs with extra chili and a *Yoo-hoo,* "the chocolate energy drink", which was water, high fructose corn syrup and cocoa. After I told everyone about meeting Bob at the diner and that I had accepted his offer to work in the Poconos that summer, they congratulated me and said I would be missed. The only one who had been to Buck Hill was Phoebe, who had spent a weekend there with her grandmother.

"You're going to love it. It's magical. The word that best describes Buck Hill would be, nostalgic. We'll come visit. I'll talk to my sister to see if she can find a place nearby for us to play. She just got fired, which is good news. Because now she has time to manage the band. She was too good for that job anyway, bunch of assholes. She was smarter than her boss and rather that

promoting her, he fired her. Go fucking figure! Two days on the job and we already have two bookings. That girl could sell ice to an Eskimo! I'll see if she can book something in the Poconos near Buck Hill Falls. Plus, she's got a van! Crazy isn't it? How things work out."

As soon as I got home I started packing. On top of a pile of T shirts and shorts was a threadbare swatch of fabric that was all that was left of my baby blanket. It kept me company throughout nursery school all the way through high school where I hid it under my pillow at night while I slept. When I heard my mother coming up the stairs, I folded it neatly into a small square and placed it carefully in the pocket of my backpack.

"Need any help?" she asked knowing what the answer would be. *"Almost done,"* I said. As I zipped my duffle bag we both sensed the transition that was taking place. For the first time in my life, I was leaving home. *"I'm really going to miss you"* she said. "*We make a pretty good team. I've done my best to be a good mom. I've made some mistakes, and I'm deeply sorry. One was not telling you more about your father. Some of the things that Bob told you. Things you should know. Those were complicated times. There are some things that still need explaining but I*

thought it would be best to wait until you were old enough to understand. Maybe then you would be able to forgive me. Now isn't really the best time to talk about it, but soon."

We got up early the next morning to pay a visit to my maternal grandfather who had been in the Veterans hospital since my grandmother passed away more than a decade ago. Even though he had dementia and hadn't spoken in almost ten years, he recognized us and looked forward to our visits. It was my mother's idea to stop by and pick him up on the way to Buck Hill Falls so he could see me before I left for the summer and he could have an outing. As we were pulling into the VA parking lot she turned to me and said, *"He's not supposed to leave the grounds, but I told them he has a doctor's appointment, so they told me they would make an exception. Just don't say anything about us driving to the Poconos."*

At the end of a long hallway that smelled like cleaning fluid and urine was a common room where a group of veterans was sitting in wheelchairs in front of a TV with the volume turned way up. Nobody seemed to be watching television and several of the men had fallen asleep and were hunched over their unfinished trays of food. It made me not want to ever get old. The only one who wasn't asleep was my grandpa who was looking out the window at some birds who had nested in the eaves. His face lit up when he saw us come into the room.

"Good morning Dad! Look who's here. Your grandson, Danny. How are we feeling today? Everything good?" Even though he didn't answer, his eyes indicated he was happy to see us.

"You have a doctor's appointment today" she said loudly enough for the nurse to hear. When he made a sad face, she whispered in his ear, *"Actually Pops, this is a jailbreak. We're kidnapping you and taking Danny to the Poconos where he will be working this summer."*

After my mom signed the release forms, I wheeled my grandfather out of the building and into the parking lot where I guided him into the front seat of our late model Chevrolet.

"It's a beautiful day and we thought you would appreciate a change of scenery." my mom said as she fastened his seatbelt. When we drove out the VA parking lot, a song by Simon *and Garfunkel* came on the radio and we became lost in the lyrics.

Let us be lovers, we'll marry our fortunes together
I've got some real estate here in my bag

So we bought a pack of cigarettes and Mrs. Wagner's pies
And we walked off to look for America

Cathy, I said as we boarded a Greyhound in Pittsburgh
Michigan seems like a dream to me now
It took me four days to hitchhike from Saginaw
I've gone to look for America...

Eventually the car dealerships and fast food restaurants were replaced by pine forests and farm stands and the gentle hum of the engine caused my Grandpa and me to fall asleep. A few miles after we pulled off the main highway, a pothole woke us up just in time to see a large sign made out of white birch tree branches that said, "WELCOME TO BUCK HILL FALLS."

"Guess we're here" I said as I yawned and attempted to rub the sleep out of my eyes. From the looks of everything we saw around us, we had somehow slipped back in time. Elegant stone cottages were tucked back into the woods and stone bridges with wrought iron lanterns arched gracefully over the narrow roads. I watched my grandpa's eyes become wide as saucers as

we drove past a horse drawn carriage and the coachman tipped his top hat to my mother.

"*What are those?*" I asked as I looked out the window out at a group of people dressed in white clothes and holding large black balls in the crooks of their arms. Pulling off to the side of the road next to a series of neatly manicured rectangular lawns, we saw a sign that told us Buck Hill Falls was the *"Site of the first US lawn bowling championships in 1931."*

As we drove up the sloping driveway to the stone Porte-Cochere entryway to the Inn, we were met by two handsome doorman wearing red and black uniforms and pillbox hats. Before the car had rolled to a stop they charged ahead and reached out to open our doors for us scaring the bejesus out of my mother.

"*We're fine*" she said as she rolled down her window. "*We can open our own doors*"

"*Of course you can*" said one of the men. "*We're just here to help. Welcome to Buck Hill Falls. Any luggage?*"

"*Unfortunately not*" my mom replied. "*We're just dropping off my son who's going to be working here this summer. I'm hoping you can help us find the administration offices?*"

"My pleasure" said the doorman. *"Just inside the reception area, past the potted palms, take a right and you'll see a bank of elevators. Meeting rooms and executive offices are located on the second floor and clearly identified. You shouldn't have any trouble finding your way. And when you get back your car will be waiting for you right here."* With a flourish of his hand he gestured to an open space between a brand new Mercedes-Benz and a Bentley convertible.

As we walked beneath the Porte-cochere we passed a woman who seemed to be in her early forties dressed like a flapper. A long strand of pearls dangled between her braless breasts and she was wearing a bell-shaped cloche hat. An unusual piece of jewelry that looked like a raven with one red bejeweled eye was pinned to her hat and she was standing in front of a sandwich board that said "MRS BURDLER'S WALKING TOURS"

"You look like a man with a curious mind!" she told my grandfather as she jabbed him repeatedly with her long black cigarette holder. When he didn't reply, she continued her pitch. *"Buck Hill was founded as a Quaker retreat. The Inn was built by a well-known architectural firm and the gardens and grounds were designed by Frederick Law Olmstead. He designed Central*

Park in New York City." When we tried to move away as quickly as my grandpa could walk, she followed us into the hotel lobby. "*Eleanor Roosevelt stayed here when she was a young woman. Do you believe in ghosts?*" she continues. "*We have several.*" As soon as we found the elevator, my mother started pressing the call button repeatedly which caused the woman to speak even more quickly. "*Ask the woman at the front desk if you can stay in room 226. It's a lovely room, but it's not available. It never is. Want to know why? Take my tour and I'll tell you the secret.*"

As soon as the elevator doors opened we piled in hoping she wouldn't follow us. "*No room*" my mother said as she positioned my grandfather directly between the woman and the closing elevator doors. Undeterred, she tried to squeeze in around him but the doors clamped shut on her waving cigarette holder locking it in place as we moved up to the second floor. The moment the doors opened it dropped to the floor and disappeared through a crack as if it had been held by ghost. "*Well, that was certainly unusual!*" commented my mother.

My mother waited outside the business office with my grandfather on a large couch in the hallway while I went inside and was introduced to a nerdy looking accountant who wore oversized glasses and a had a gold chain around his neck with a tiny gold medallion. When I told him my name and mentioned that Bob Robertson had offered me a job as at the camp he didn't seem to have a clue about who I was or what I was talking about.

"I wouldn't worry about it." he reassured me. *"That's pretty much business as usual around this place these days. Fill out these forms, we'll figure it out later."* After I completed the forms, he walked me back to his desk which was overflowing with bills and invoices, and gave me a green punch card that would allow me to eat at the employee cafeteria. On his desk was a nameplate that said "John Valhakus" and a picture of an attractive young girl standing in front of a dark green 1973 Pontiac Firebird. I wasn't sure if he needed anything else from me so I thanked him and said, *"Well, it was nice to meet you, John."*

"Nobody calls me John" he replied. *"Call me Q. First letter of my middle name. There were so many kids in Catholic school named John, my teacher started calling me Q, and it stuck. Look, you seem like a nice kid, so I'll give you some advice. This place might look like a pretty smooth operation but financially, it's a mess. It costs a bloody fortune to run a place like this and every*

year people have more and more vacation options to choose from. So soon as someone hands you a paycheck, run over to the bank and cash it. Don't wait for the ink to dry."

Before I left, I turned and said, *"Nice car. Is that your daughter?"* The look on Q's face told me I'd made another mistake and I wished I had never opened my mouth.

"Good God, I hope not! She's my girlfriend. She's older than she looks. She's 22 and I just turned 35. So there's a gap, but we share a love for fast cars. Her parents own a cottage here, so she is what we call a "Cottager". Before I got here, the Cottagers co-signed a loan to keep this place afloat. When things didn't turn around fast enough, they refused to pay more than what they felt was their 'fair share'. Come September, the bank could end up owning this place."

While we were talking, a man wearing an ill-fitting suit kept looking over suspiciously. Finally he walked over, gave me a nod and told Q it was time for him to get back to work.

"Who was that?" I asked after the man had gone back inside his glass office.

"Management," Q muttered. *"The guy who is supposed to have all the answers. Been here almost eight months and he can't figure out how to find the goddamn men's room!"*

Outside the Administration offices, an elderly woman with a four pronged cane and an ear horn was asking my grandfather where he had served during "The Great War."

"Please stop shouting," my mother begged the woman. *"He's not deaf, he's mute. He can hear what you are saying, he's just unable to answer. It was nice of you to stop by, but it would be better for everyone if you would please kindly move along."*

After she made an unhappy face and uttered something that sounded like *'harrumph'* she wobbled away down the long carpeted hallway beneath a row of cut crystal chandeliers.

"What's up with this place?" my mom said. *"People are friendly. Almost too friendly. Someone should tell that poor woman they have these things called 'hearing aids'. They fit right inside your ear. How did it go in there? Are you all signed up?"*

After I told her I was all set, we decided to take the stairs down to lobby and try to find Cottage 16 that Bob had talked about without crossing paths with the flapper or the crone.

"That must be it" my mother said pointing to a three-story shingled cottage in the woods behind the Inn. Coming around to the front of the building, we saw a weathered Subaru with Colorado plates that was covered with pine needles and looked like it might have been there all winter. When I knocked on the door beside the garage, it swung open on rusty hinges and we found ourselves looking up a dark winding staircase with no windows.

"Hello. Mr. Snow? Anyone home?" I shouted into the stairwell. When no one answered, I grabbed my suitcase, backpack and pillow and the three of us trudged up the creaking steps until we finally reached what we assumed was the third floor. Out of breath from the climb, we noticed a pungent odor. It wasn't the typical summer cottage smell of Pine Sol and wet wool, it was something different. *"What's on earth is that smell?"* my mother complained. *"It must be a skunk. Or something dead. Or a dead skunk."* When I looked down the darkened staircase at Grandpa Joe, I noticed he was pinching his nose trying not to breathe in the terrible stench.

Emerging from the darkness, we suddenly came face to face with a bearded man who was wearing a long white robe.

He seemed to be in his late twenties or early thirties and my first thought was that Rip Van Winkle must be the homeless guy who belonged to the Subaru parked downstairs. For some reason he was holding his breath and his eyes were beginning to bulge out. Slowly, he raised his arms and struck a pose that was very similar to Jesus Christ nailed to the cross. Finally, unable to hold his breath any longer, he exhaled a tremendous cloud of pungent white smoke and coughed loudly three times.

"Holy smokes!" bellowed my grandfather. *"Did I die? Lord, where is my wife? Gloria? Come to me sweetheart. I miss you so much!"*

Shocked beyond belief, my mother exclaimed, *"It's a miracle! He hasn't said a word in almost ten years. Who are you? And what are you doing up here?"*

When he didn't answer, I looked around and saw a *Sony Walkman* and headphones next to a large red water pipe on the floor. Suddenly, I remembered we didn't see a number on the cottage. We must have wandered into the wrong house at precisely the wrong moment.

"We are deeply sorry!" I apologized. *"We thought we were in Cottage 16, and I called up but I guess you didn't hear us. So*

if you will please accept our sincerest apologies, we will retrace our steps and be on our way. We are sorry to have troubled you."

"No trouble at all." the man said. *"I just kind of feel sorry for you, having walked up all those stairs in the dark. Been meaning to replace the bulb. But there's something about what you said that doesn't make sense. You said you were looking for Cottage 16. Well, this is Cottage 16. So either you, or the person who sent you here are wrong. Which do you think it is?"*

After I told him that Bob Robertson had told me to go to Cottage 16, I asked him if he knew a person named Julian Snow, and if so, would he be willing to tell us his whereabouts?

"Well, that brings up another curious question." he said, raking his fingers through his long beard. *"Because, I happen to know Julian quite well. But before I tell you where to find him, I should probably ask about the nature of your visit. Is it personal or business?"*

"Business" I told him. *"A friend of ours, actually an acquaintance, who owns a cottage here, offered me a job at the camp that Mr. Snow is in charge of and said I could live with him at Cottage 16. So if you could just point us in the right direction, we will be on our way."*

"Of course" he said. *"But before I do, I was just wondering if Julian was expecting you? Did you speak to him about this job and your living arrangements? From what I've heard, Mr. Snow has a reputation of being a loner who greatly appreciates his privacy."*

"He very well might be. I really have no idea." I said. *"We've actually never met or even spoken. I guess I should have called, but Mr. Robertson told me to get here as soon as possible. He said he would speak to Mr. Snow and that everything would be fine. So I believed him and quit my job back home and we drove up here this morning. When I stopped by the Inn they had no idea who I was and now I'm beginning to wonder if this is all a big misunderstanding. So if you won't tell us how to find Mr. Snow, we should probably circle back to Mr. Robertson and try figure out what's going on. Once again, we are sorry for the intrusion."*

"Stop saying you're sorry." he said. *"It's not your fault. It sounds like you were just doing what someone told you to do. You trusted this Mr. Robertson and he has clearly let you down. But there's no reason for everyone to get uptight. I understand, uptightness happens. But now that I'm familiar with your plight, I might be able to offer you some assistance. But before I do that,*

it would be helpful for me to know everyone's name, since we've just met and we haven't been properly introduced."

After I introduced my mother and grandfather, I told him I was Daniel Patrick Barnes who just graduated from high school in Allentown, Pennsylvania where I had a job at *The Hardware Depot,* until yesterday when I abruptly quit and turned in my nametag and apron and I was going to be a freshman at *William and Mary* in September. He seemed mildly interested in my story and nodded almost imperceptibly when I was finished. Then, he turned to my mother and my grandfather and asked them if I had been a good kid. Unfortunately, my grandfather never spoke again after his near transcendental experience at the top of the stairs, but he nodded his head in agreement as my mother told Grizzly Adams that I had never given her any trouble growing up and how proud she was of me.

"Well that's great to hear." he said. *"By the time most kids are done being teenagers, their parents want to throw them out the second story window. I know mine did. It took a while, but we're friends again. So now that I know who you are, I should probably introduce myself."*

"I'm Julian Snow. For the record, I've never heard from anyone named Bob Robertson and have no idea who he is. But the good news is, even though we just met, I happen to like you. And now that I've heard your story, and met your mother who seems like a trustworthy person, I feel confident that I can offer you a position at Camp Club for the summer. Good organizations always find room for good people."

As for the living arrangements, what I mentioned earlier is true. I've always been a lone wolf and I appreciate my privacy. However, this is a large house and there's an empty bedroom across the hall, so we should be able to cohabitate without interfering with the rhythms of our daily lives. If not, I can make other arrangements so you will have a roof over your head. But before you move in, there's one more question I should probably ask. Have you ever served time and if so what was the nature of your offense and how recently were you incarcerated."

"Wait a minute. I don't understand?" my mother said. *"Are you asking my son if he has ever been in prison?"*

"Yes, exactly." said Julian. *"Since he would be working with children, I have to make sure they are safe under his care and supervision. And secondly, if your son has spent time recently in*

prison for a minor felony, say petty larceny, we would qualify for a 'work opportunity tax credit' of $2,400 for hiring workers with past felonies. That would pretty much cover the cost of hiring him. Plus, I'm sure your son would have some pretty interesting stories."

"The answer is no" my mother said emphatically. *"My son has never served time"*

"Fine." said Julian. *"I won't hold that against him. We operate on a tight budget, so I just thought I should ask. Camp club operates Monday through Friday from 8:00 in the morning until 4:00 in the afternoon and is available to children of families who own cottages, as well as the children of hotel guests between the ages of 8 and 14. Pay is $200 a week, plus room and board. I hold a staff meeting every weekday morning at 7:30 and you are free to spend your evenings and weekends however you choose."*

"As an employee of the Inn you are permitted to eat in the company cafeteria, but I don't recommend it. We had a nasty salmonella outbreak last week. Nobody's sure where it came from. Succotash is my guess. Which must be Spanish for Salmonella. My bowels are still barking. This place has only has one bathroom, so don't be shy about using the air freshener. Your

room is down the hall on the left so if you will please excuse me, it's time for my daily meditation."

As I unpacked my clothes and put them in the dresser next to the bed, my mom found the picture of her that was in my locker in high school and taped it to a mirror on the wall.

"*So you will think of me*" she said as she looked over sadly. All the excitement of the day had completely exhausted my grandfather who had fallen asleep on the bed. "*I'd like to stay, but I need to return your grandfather before someone reports him missing.*"

A gentle rain was starting to fall when my mother came back with the car. By that time, it was next to impossible to wake my sleeping grandfather, so the two of us had to practically carry him down the dark staircase in order to slide him into the front seat of the waiting car. Anyone walking by could have easily believed we were two perpetrators removing a body from a crime scene. After we said goodbye and my mother dried her eyes, I climbed back up to my room on the third floor and ate a baloney sandwich and some Mott's Applesauce my mother had packed for me that morning. After that I lay on my bed and tried to read a book but ended up falling asleep to the hypnotic sounds of Buddhist chanting coming from Julian's bedroom.

That night I had a dream that I was walking down the hallway of a haunted hotel. Behind each door I heard a different set of scary sounds: unintelligible whispering, a couple having an argument, a woman sobbing and a deep, almost sexual, moaning. At the end of the hallway was room 226; the one the tour guide had talked about. As I got closer, I noticed the door had been left partially open and the sound of a steady drumbeat was coming from inside the room.

"Thump, thump, thump."

Curious to know what or who was making the strange drumming sound, I pushed open the door and slipped inside. The room was decorated in the Victorian style with curved couches covered in smooth red velvet. There were mirrors on the walls but none of them seemed to be able to reflect my image. As I moved across the room past elaborate Tiffany lamps, I noticed a sculpture of a black raven with one red bejeweled eye like the brooch the tour guide had been wearing. Over the fireplace was an oil painting of a woman and a young girl standing on the banks of a swollen river just about to overflow.

They were wearing long dresses and holding parasols. Just as I was about to I look away, the girl in the picture seemed to see me in the room and let go of her parasol which was carried away by a sudden gust of wind. After it disappeared, she started waving her arms frantically in the air as if trying to warn me about something. And that was when I heard her talk. At first, I couldn't understand what she was saying, but when she began repeating it over and over it was unmistakable.

"Go back!" she said. *"You don't belong here."* Unable to follow her advice, I made my way slowly toward the interior bedroom door where the "*thump, thump, thump.*" was getting progressively louder. When I came to the threshold of the bedroom door, I took a deep breath and with one finger pushed the door open a crack so I could see inside. Sitting on the floor, with his back to me, was a young boy wearing overalls banging on a small tin drum. I couldn't see his face, but I desperately needed to know who he was, so I tiptoed closer until I was standing right behind him. Not wanting to startle him, I reached down and put my hand on his shoulder which caused him to stop. Suddenly there was a tremendous explosion and I woke up in a cold sweat not knowing where I was. Outside my

window a steady rain was coming down and I heard the sound of thunder rumbling far off in the distance. Relieved, I rubbed the sleep out of my eyes and sat up in bed and told myself that it was just a bad dream and that everything was fine. But, then, why did I still hear that steady drumbeat? Was it coming from Julian's room? Cautiously, I pulled off the covers and crawled out of my bed and walked slowly down the dark hallway. The closer I got to the bathroom, the louder the sound got. "*thump, thump, thump.*" Pushing the bathroom door open a crack with my finger, exactly as I had done in the dream, I peered inside and saw a small metal trash can catching drops of rainwater dripping from a crack in the ceiling. Julian must have known there was a leak and positioned the trash can there during the night.

Since there was no possibility of me getting back to sleep that night, I got dressed and got ready for our morning staff meeting. A previous resident had left a promotional brochure on the coffee table in the living room and when I opened it up I saw a map of the grounds and some pictures of the golf course, a ski slope and a cascading waterfall where a fisherman had just caught what looked like a rainbow trout. Below the Inn, at the foot of a hill was a small log cabin next to a playground and a baseball diamond and a carved sign that said "CAMP CLUB".

I'd forgotten to bring a raincoat, so I found a large trash bag in the kitchen and cut a few holes in the corners and made a slit on top so I could wear it as a poncho. It wasn't great, but I figured it was better than nothing. Julian must have gotten up early that morning because he was gone by the time I slipped out the door and walked through the woods to Camp Club.

The log cabin was smaller than it looked in the brochure, but was cozy and comfortable. When I got there, Julian was sitting at a small desk writing something down on a clipboard. The fact that he was surrounded by a group of drowsy-looking counselors and had a whistle hanging from his neck gave him the appearance of being a cabin leader and not a religious figure. It was then that I first began to realize that Julian was what some people would call a "chameleon."

"Good morning! I want to thank everyone for getting here early. I know it wasn't easy getting up on a day like this, but the weather is supposed to clear up soon. It's nice to see so many familiar faces, and a few new recruits. Joining us for the first time is Daniel Barnes who is going to be paired off with Veronica

Voss. The two of you will in charge of junior boys and junior girls. Maeve and Parker did such a good job with Intermediate campers last year it would have been impossible to replace them with anyone better, so they're back for another tour of duty. Welcome! And the dynamic duo Molly and Garrett have teamed up to try to take on the challenges of our senior boys and girls. I have complete confidence in you both and know that you will do an exceptional job this year.

It's a pleasure to see the lovely and talented Mary-Cait behind the easel once again as head of Arts and Crafts. And since no human being has spent more time at Camp Club than Tommy Collins, he will be a Counselor in Training, a CIT, also known as a 'Floater'. So if any of you need a personal day, an extra pair of hands, eyes or ears talk to me and Tommy will be glad to help you out. Tommy, thank you for your service."

As Julian laid out the game plan for the week ahead, Veronica came over and sat down next to me. She was average height, like me, with shoulder length auburn hair and hazel eyes with flecks of amber and green. A moment or so later she whispered, *"Whoever you are, thank you."*

"Thank you for what?" I asked.

"For saving me from a summer in 'Tommy-land'. He's a nice kid, but he takes everything way too seriously. I mean, we're camp counselors. We're not neuro-surgeons. This is supposed to be fun. Julian had me paired up with Tommy until you showed up. So I hope you're fun."

"I'll try." I said. *"But I have to warn you. I'm a neuro-surgeon."*

"Are you kidding? You're kidding, right?

"I'm kidding."

"Thank God! As long as you have a sense of humor, we'll get along just fine."

When Veronica saw that it was after 8:00 and Julian was still rambling on, she raised her hand and said, *"Excuse me. Mr. Snow. I know you have a lot of important things to say, but it's raining, and the kids are here, so maybe we should open the door and let them come inside?"*

"Right you are" said Julian, looking up from his clipboard and noticing the campers faces pressed up against the glass of the windows. *"Let summer begin!"*

The last camper to arrive was Briny Bell who was accompanied by his young attractive mother whose given name was Liberty Bell, but to her friends she was known simply as Libby. Whenever someone asked her about her name she explained that her parents had named her after a mountain in Washington State that her father, a world-renowned rock climber, had conquered when his wife was pregnant and not *"that cracked thing in Philadelphia"*. She was right but she was also wrong, because the mountain her father had scaled without using ropes was shaped like a bell and had been named for *"that cracked thing in Philadelphia."*

Standing just inside the Camp Club doorway to get out of the rain, Mrs. Bell was wearing a skimpy tennis outfit that was now completely soaked and revealed more of the contours of her body than anyone, with the possible exception of her husband, was accustomed to seeing.

"Briny and I got caught in the rain", she said unnecessarily.

"I'm so sorry" said Julian. *"C'mon inside. Maybe there's something we can dry you off with? Danny, hand me that box of tee shirts. Here."* he said, holding up a tiny yellow tee shirt with the words "CAMP CLUB" and an image of a roaring campfire printed on the front.

"It's a size small, but we have plenty of mediums, if you'd be more comfortable?

"It's fine" she said. *"I'm not going to be wearing it, but I will use it to dry off."*

After she dried herself off and tried to hand it back to Julian, he told her she could keep it and said he thought it would look great on her. I don't think he was intentionally trying to flirt with her, but that was the way it came across and after he said it she turned and blushed.

The sun finally came out around 10:00 and after the puddles had dried up on the playing fields we moved outside and formed a circle around the flagpole to sing the Camp Club song. Everyone but me knew the words by heart, so Veronica wrote them down on a scrap of paper.

We welcome you to Camp Club
and we're mighty glad you're here.
We'll sing the air reverberating
with a mighty CHEER!
We'll sing you in, we'll sing you out
and you will raise a mighty SHOUT!
Hail, hail, the gang's all here
and you're welcome to Buck Hill Falls!

The first day of camp was filled with a never ending series of the usual camp activities including capture the flag, archery, arts and crafts and the dreaded swim test that took place in the Olympic-sized outdoor swimming pool that was a short walk from the Inn. Since the pool had just been filled a few days ago, the water was a brisk 56 degrees and Veronica and I had a difficult time trying to coax our collection of skinny eight year olds into the freezing water. We drew straws to decide which one of us was going to dive in to demonstrate it was survivable. I lost, but when Veronica saw how apprehensive I was about going in the water, she stripped off her hooded sweatshirt and without hesitation dove into the deep end. After the last camper had demonstrated the ability to float, swim or dog paddle to the side of the pool, she emerged from the icy water and as I handed her a towel I noticed her lips were purple.

By the end of the day we were both completely exhausted and so were our campers. Noticing several of my boys had fallen asleep beneath the ferns that were growing by the side of the pool, Veronica said *"Three sleepers. Nice job. Their parents will be happy when they get home and pass out. My girls are still going strong. But girls are much heartier than boys. It's biologically proven. We have more stamina. Not that it's a competition, but if it was, we would win. So, tell me Danny. What's your story? I mean, how did you end up here?"*

Taking a deep breath, I decided to give her the short version of how I ended up at Buck Hill. "*It's actually pretty random. On my 18th birthday I got a letter from an lawyer named Bob Robertson who owns a cottage here, and he told me he had something that he needed to tell me about my father, who disappeared shortly after I was born. We met for breakfast, he told me a few things that I didn't know and said there was a job opening at camp club this summer. Which technically wasn't true. But when I met Julian at Cottage 16 he took pity on me and offered me a job which is how Tommy Collins became a 'floater' and you ended up with me.*"

"Your father 'disappeared'? Or did he just go somewhere? Like, he hit the road?"

"No. He actually disappeared. He went on a business trip and never came back. I was a baby, so all I know is what other people have told me, and nobody seems to know much. My mom didn't remarry, so it's been just the two of us for the last 18 years. Like

I said, it's pretty random how I got here. But I'm glad it worked out. What about you? How'd you end up here?"

"I came here for the weekend with a friend from school. She went to Camp Club when she was a kid and I reminded her of her favorite counselor. They don't come here anymore, but she helped me fill out an application and I got the job. This is my third summer. It's a nice break from school. No pressure. Weekends off. I grew up in an apartment in Philadelphia, which was nice, but I appreciate being out here in the boonies. The kids are great. They're the right age and up for just about anything. Two years from now their hormones will kick in and they will get a little crazy. I know I did. Wouldn't want to do that again. Drove my mom right to the edge of a cliff. Somehow we both survived. There's something about mothers and daughters, but I don't want to get into that. Not now, maybe never. We're best friends now. Unlike boys, most women are able to fight and forgive. It would be nice if we could forget, but two out of three isn't bad."

When I got back to Cottage 16 that afternoon I figured it was time to give Mr. Robertson a call and try to find out why he hadn't contacted Julian about me working there that summer. I was supposed to give him a call on Sunday afternoon, but there had been so much going on that day I forgot. After I located the scrap of paper he had given me at breakfast, I found a black rotary phone beneath the sofa in the living room and dialed the number he had given me. It rang and rang and I tried calling several times but nobody answered. Finally it dawned on me that it was Monday and he was probably back in Philadelphia, so found the certified letter he had sent and dialed the main number of the law firm where he worked. After being politely asked to hold three times, he finally picked up the call and asked how I was.

"I'm doing fine Mr. Robertson" I said.

"Where are you?" he asked. *"When I didn't hear from you I thought you backed out."*

"I'm at Buck Hill. In Cottage 16, where you told me to go."

"Wonderful! Then I'm glad to hear things worked out."

"I met Mr. Snow. He said nobody contacted him, about me working here."

"Well, it wasn't for lack of trying! Mr. Snow doesn't seem to know how to answer his own damn phone. And since you seem to be calling from his phone, it's obviously operational. I'm hoping he was able offer you a position doing something productive?"

"He did. At Camp club. I'm the junior boys counselor."

"Well done! Listen Danny, I want to hear all about this, but I'm in the middle of a trial, so let's get together Friday night at my place for dinner. If you're a vegetarian, try to get over it by the end of the week because we're having steak. See you at 7:00."

After I hung up I decided to take a look around Cottage 16. People were starting to talk about a new decorating style called "Shabby Chic", which was just another way of saying "old and worn out". Most of the furniture looked like it might have fallen off a truck on the way to the dump and been hastily repaired. The rugs were stained and threadbare and the pictures looked like they had might have been purchased at a flea market. The best thing you could say about the lamps was that they worked. A few even had light bulbs. I had no idea where Julian was but his bedroom door was partially open, so I decided to take a quick look inside.

Julian had what looked like a Navajo blanket on his bed, which was neatly made. On the wall was a large tapestry of a naked three-eyed Buddhist goddess. Next to his bed were several candles and a stack of books, most of which I had never heard of. *The Tibetan Book of the Dead* and *The Wisdom of Insecurity* by Alan Watts as well as *Factotum* by Charles Bukowski. On the window ledge was a record player and *Adagio in G* by *Tomaso Albinoni* was on the turntable stacked on top of *Blood on the Tracks* by Bob Dylan. Leaning against the wall was a guitar and a small, oddly-shaped case with a handle that looked like it might contain a French horn.

My first week as a camp counselor was almost seamless thanks to Veronica. Since I had never been to camp, and had no idea about the traditions the kids looked forward to all year, she explained everything to me and I went along with whatever she said. Our schedules were well planned out by Julian and the other counselors and it was our job to make sure the kids were kept busy and entertained so their parents could have some time to themselves. Most of the campers were children of Cottagers who lived in the homes surrounding the Inn but a big part of our job was introducing the children of the hotel guests to the other kids and making sure they felt included and accepted. It really wasn't that difficult. At the end of the day it was an amazing feeling to see a kid who'd been alone and intimidated that morning walk back to the Inn surrounded by a group of kids acting like they were going to be friends for life.

It was a short walk to Bob's cottage and it was starting to get dark outside so I could see inside the houses along the way. People were going about their evening routines. Unlike where I grew up; where people mostly sat alone in darkened living rooms worshipping the dancing blue light of their television sets, people at Buck Hill were sitting in their living rooms reading biographies or novels recommended by friends or the *New York Times Best Seller list*. The only sound that night was the sound of my footsteps on the smooth pavement and the breezes that whispered through the trees above my head collecting the sharp, refreshing scent of pine and blending it with the damp mossy aroma of vegetation coming from the surrounding woods. When I reached the stone bridge, the cast iron lamps on both sides took on the appearance of palace guards holding out their lanterns to illuminate the way for horse drawn carriages.

Bob Robertson's cottage was a white clapboard colonial with a dark green shutters set back in the woods away from the street behind a low rock wall. As I walked up the curving path to his front door, I saw there were lights on in the kitchen and I could hear what sounded like big band music coming from inside his house. After I rang the doorbell, I heard footsteps and he greeted me at the door wearing a chef's apron and holding a very large cocktail.

"Good timing!" he said. *"Welcome. C'mon in my boy. Let's get a drink in your hands. I'm having gin, but you can have whatever you want. Please, make yourself at home."* When I told him I'd like a ginger ale, he added two jiggers of dark rum and a half a lime to make something he told me he once had at the *Royal Bermuda Yacht Club* called a *Dark & Stormy.*

"Keeps the scurvy away." he said handing me the drink in an oversized glass that matched his own and looked like it could possibly have been an ice bucket. When he saw my reluctance to take the enormous cocktail, he told me that his doctor had recommended he limit his alcohol consumption to *two* drinks per day, so he bought all new barware.

"Don't be shy, lad. Take it. Use both hands if you have to. I need to check on our steaks." While he grilled the steaks in the backyard, we talked about my encounter with Julian and what had happened during my first week as a camp counselor. When I told him the last names of some of my campers he seemed to know just about everyone and told me some interesting

stories about where their money came from and things that had happened in the past.

As interesting as the stories were, the only ones I really wanted to hear were the ones about my father. Stories that revealed what kind of a person he was. Was my father anxious and introspective like me, or was he self-confident and an extrovert? Was he good at telling jokes? Did he have a sense of humor? What color were his eyes? There were so many things I desperately wanted to know that my mother hadn't been able to talk about.

The steaks were delicious and Bob had cooked them perfectly. We started out talking about me but the conversation always seemed to revert back to him. Bob enjoyed talking about Bob. He was 45 years old and by all accounts was a successful and well-respected attorney. He never married, but had come close on several occasions. During the past twenty five years, Bob appeared to have dated almost every single available woman who spent an appreciable amount of time at Buck Hill. Remarkably, after each breakup, they remained the best of friends.

My guess was Bob's doctor hadn't explained that a glass of wine was pretty much the same as a cocktail because after we finished the first bottle of red wine he pulled the cork on another, and refilled our glasses. When I mentioned I was underage, because the drinking age in Pennsylvania was 21, he scoffed, "*Nonsense. Buck Hill doesn't have a drinking age. What might be true for the great state of Pennsylvania, doesn't apply here. You're not driving and 'a pleasure shared is a pleasured doubled!' I settled a big court case today and we have reason to celebrate. A friend of mine owed me a favor and I found a way to thank Mr. Snow for hiring you and made camp club the recipient of my friend's generosity. 'Quid pro quo'. That's Latin for 'a favor for a favor'. I'm not at liberty to tell you what the favor is, but I assure you, you will both be pleasantly surprised.*"

After dinner I helped clear the table and we sat in the living room while he told stories about my father. Apparently my father did have a sense of humor, because when he and Bob were at Princeton they removed one of the toilets from the bathroom in an exclusive dining club and cemented it to the chimney on the roof during the night. The next morning, when everyone was walking to class they saw a mannequin dressed like one of their least favorite professors sitting on the commode on top of the building reading a book on philosophy.

It was starting to get late and when I returned from using the bathroom I noticed Bob had fallen asleep on the couch and was snoring loudly. I tried to wake him, but nothing seemed to work and I was worried because he was still clutching a large glass of red wine. Wondering what to do, I decided to try to pry his fingers from the wine glass so it wouldn't spill on the tan carpet or brightly colored floral print sofa. Not wanting to startle him, I sat down on the sofa and grasped his wine glass firmly in my left hand while I used my other hand to pull his fingers from around the narrow stem of the wine glass, one finger at a time. The only problem was, as soon as I would get one or two fingers away from the fragile stem they would slowly curl back around and I would have to start all over. More than once he seemed to be waking up, but after several minutes I was finally able to free the glass from his grip and set it down safely on the kitchen counter. By the time I got back to the living room, I noticed he seemed to be having a pleasant dream on the sofa, so I scribbled a thank you note and left it on the breakfast table, where I hoped he would see it in the morning, and slipped quietly out the front door.

I had no plans that weekend so I stopped by the girls cottage to see what Veronica was up to. She was in the kitchen, still in her pajamas, when I knocked on the front door and she invited me in for coffee. While she ate cereal and I drank my Nescafe instant coffee she told me about some of the things going on nearby.

"There's really not much of a town. We have a bowling alley, a Mexican restaurant and a lesbian biker bar. If that's not your thing, there's a great Italian restaurant called Maccioni's on route 302 where they make the most amazing Penne alla vodka. The Pocono Playhouse is in Mountainhome and they have a few good concerts and one or two shows practicing their lines on their way to Broadway. Other than the honeymoon resorts and sports camps the Pocono's is known for, you have to go all the way to Stroudsburg to find any nightlife or singles bars."

After she went upstairs and got dressed, Veronica drove me around in her Toyota Corolla and showed me some of the places she had talked about, including *Mount Airy lodge* where she told me the rooms all had heart shaped bathtubs. She didn't seem to appreciate it when I asked her if she knew this from personal experience. If parts of the Catskills could be described as *The Borscht Belt,* parts of the Pocono's could certainly be called *The Kitsch belt.* Souvenir shops, ice cream parlors and confectionary destinations with names like *Callie's Candy Kitchen* dotted the landscape of the rural highways. From what Veronica told me, the Pocono's attracted an interesting mix of people from swinging singles to newlyweds and families. Avid sportsmen and recent immigrants bought their groceries from the same market as wealthy Quakers and the descendants of Jewish socialists.

When I got to Camp Club on Monday morning for the staff meeting, I noticed something unusual. A white bus from *the Pennsylvania Department of Corrections* was parked directly in front of the log cabin. Nobody was sitting in the driver's seat and, as far as I could tell, there were no inmates, unless they were hiding under their seats. The door to the bus had been left open, so I took a look inside and saw the keys hanging in the ignition and realized the engine was running. When I walked inside Camp Club, I saw Julian sitting at his desk looking worried.

"I have no idea what that thing is doing here. I called security and they are on their way. I took a look around, but couldn't find anyone. No driver, no inmates. Why don't you check Arts & Crafts and make sure nobody is hiding in the supply closet That's the only place I didn't look. Actually, never mind. Security can handle that. They should be here any minute."

When security showed up they told Julian to stop worrying. Escaped inmates were not hiding in the woods behind Camp Club. Apparently, someone had made arrangements for the bus to be donated to the camp so we could take the kids on day trips and excursions. Whoever it was didn't have time to get the bus repainted. When Julian pressed the officer about who had donated the bus, and why he hadn't been notified, the man told him the individual wished to remain anonymous. When Julian started to get frustrated with the officer, I waved him off.

"I think I know who did this." I told him. *"I'll explain later, after they leave."*

As soon as they left, I told Julian about my dinner with Bob Robertson on Friday night and the "surprise" he had talked about. Even though I hardly knew Mr. Robertson at all, it certainly seemed like something he was capable of doing.

All Julian could say *was "I can't wait to meet this friend of yours. He sounds like quite a character. We need to get that rig out of here before it scares the campers away. Ever driven a bus?"* When I shook my head and said *"Nope"* he said *"Well, no time like the present.* After I ground the gears and stalled twice, I was finally able to maneuver the bus into the woods behind the maintenance facility that was next to Camp Club.

The following week turned out to be one of the hottest on record and we spent a lot of time at the pool having a mini-Olympics and sitting in the shade provided by the tall oak trees that circled the perimeter. In between events, Veronica and I had a lot of time to talk and get to know each other better. She was a sophomore at Vanderbilt, which was in Nashville, studying political science and thinking about going to law school. She had always been a good debater, which some people misinterpreted as having an argumentative streak. She seemed to have an opinion on just about everything, but she also was a patient listener when someone expressed an opinion that was different from her own. *"That's fascinating"* she would say when she heard something she didn't agree with or understand. *"I understand where you are coming from, but I'm not sure I agree with you."* We both were comfortable in each other's silences.

After the third straight day of record breaking heat, the kids had accumulated so many aluminum foil swimming medals everyone looked like Mark Spitz after the 1972 Olympics in Munich. The sun had scorched the playing fields, which had become hard as cement, and it was too hot for Arts & Crafts which was indoors with only a small oscillating fan to push the warm air around.

Finally Veronica remembered the waterfall. We weren't supposed to go there, because it was technically on private property, but people had been going there for years and nobody had ever been asked to leave. When she brought it up, I said there were only two problems: How we were going to get there, and what about the steep, winding path that went from the parking area down to the waterfall itself. All the kids could swim, but the rocks were slippery and we would have to be extra careful to make sure nobody fell and got hurt.

"We'll take the bus!" Veronica said. *"Somebody drove it here, so it obviously works. We can take that. And we'll rope the kids together on the path down to the waterfall. It's not that steep,*

but I'm sure they would find that exciting! Make an adventure out of it."

When I told her I wasn't keen on driving the bus and we would have to ask Julian for permission, she told me not to worry about Julian. *"Julian won't be a problem. Trust me. I can convince Julian to do whatever I want. So all you need to do is figure out how to drive the bus. How hard could that be? It's just like a car, only longer."*

"A lot longer with a 6 speed gearbox and buttons that appear to be in Russian."

"You'll figure it out" she said. *"I have confidence in you. Go practice. I'll watch the kids."*

Reluctantly, I walked behind the maintenance building and saw the bus parked where I had left it earlier in the week with the keys still in the ignition. I searched under the seat and in a small compartment next to the gearbox for a manual, but couldn't find anything. Pulling out the choke I primed the engine and when I turned the key the engine roared to life. Next to the choke was a button labeled "THROTTLE" but I had no idea what it was for, so I left it alone.

Once I got used to the gearshift, driving the bus wasn't that difficult. I brought it out to the roads surrounding the golf course where I practiced not rolling backwards on hills. I learned it was better to keep the bus in gear and engaged on a hill rather than coming to a complete stop. If I got into trouble, I knew I could always reach down and pull the emergency brake. By the time I got back to Camp Club I noticed I had put more than 40 miles on the odometer.

Julian said 'yes' to Veronica, but told her we needed to get permission slips from all the parents allowing their children to ride on the bus and for us to bring them to the waterfall. A few kids simply didn't show up, but most of them did and when we pulled out of Camp Club that morning nearly every seat on the bus was occupied by a kid with a backpack.

Indian Ladder Falls, also known as Hornbeck's Creek, was only 6 miles away from Buck Hill and a straight shot north on route 390. It took just under fifteen minutes to get there and thankfully there was a large parking lot where I could park facing outward, because I still hadn't been able to put the bus in reverse. As soon as we got there the kids piled out and Veronica and I looked at a trail map to find the best way to get to the falls. There were actually several sets of waterfalls, including one that was over fifty feet tall. We planned to hike past that one and make our way downstream where there was another set of smaller waterfalls that few people knew about where we could swim and have lunch on the warm rocks. Veronica had brought a long rope that the kids could hang onto in case one of them lost their footing on the slippery pine needles. The rope was really unnecessary, because at almost every turn there was a railing made out of repurposed branches for people to grab onto should they lose their balance.

As we snaked our way along the largely deserted trail, the loud roar we heard when we walked above the upper falls dissipated and soon we were surrounded by the low, burbling sound of water rushing over the rocks and sticks in the river below. The only part of the trail that was a bit tricky was the last twenty feet or so where the slope was steep and the soil eroded. Thinking quickly, Veronica took the rope and tied it to the base of a tree next to the trail and slid down the slope to the banks of the river where she fastened the other end to a fallen log. That way, the kids would have something to hold onto as they made their way to the natural pool that had formed in the river at the bottom of a small waterfall.

The water was cold but everyone got used to it pretty quickly and it was a welcome relief from the heat that we had been experiencing all week. The rocks were slippery and we had to constantly remind the kids to be careful as they took turns sliding down a mossy chute over a six foot waterfall into a plunge pool filled with bubbles. After everyone had cooled off, we ate our lunches on the warm rocks next to the river and stared up between the pine trees trying to identify animals in the shapes of the clouds as they drifted slowly across the sky.

The drive home on the bus was almost as exciting, in a different way, as the trip to the waterfall. I almost drove off the road when I looked in the mirror and saw Briny holding up what looked like a long knife made from a scrap of metal and a roll of duct tape.

"Look what I found!" he shouted.

Almost immediately, the rest of the kids began digging under their seats and pulling apart sections of the bus searching for similar weapons.

"It's a shank!" one of the girls said. *"Or a shiv? I'm not sure which?"*

"What's it for?" Briny asked.

"It's for stabbing people, stupid."

As soon as Briny started making stabbing gestures toward the girl, Veronica jumped up out of her seat and stumbled to the back of the bus to retrieve the weapon.

"No stabbing!" she said *"Put that down right now!"* When Briny saw she was serious, he dropped the knife on the floor causing me to hit the brakes which propelled the knife the entire length of the bus finally impaling itself in the back of my seat. Words cannot adequately describe the sound made by a group eight year olds screaming at the top of their lungs as a whirling prison knife clattered beneath their seats on the floor of a rapidly moving vehicle.

After we dropped everyone off in front of camp club, I parked the bus back behind the maintenance facility and Veronica and I spent the better part of an hour trying to find any additional concealed weapons. It they were there, they were very well hidden because we couldn't find anything. After we were both satisfied the bus was 'clean' I walked her home and trudged up the hill to Cottage 16 behind the Inn where Julian was in the living room playing his guitar. He was actually pretty good. I didn't recognize the tune but he seemed to be trying to figure out a bridge to go between a verse and the chorus. He laughed when I told him about the knife that Briny had found tucked up inside the back one of the seats.

"Guess your friend didn't do a thorough inspection. I hope he didn't steal it. Maybe we should check with the prison to see if they are aware of a missing bus?"

As Julian sat cross-legged on the floor working on the bridge, I told him about the trip to the waterfall and said we needed to do something about the signage on the bus if we were going to continue using it. He said he would call Carl in maintenance first thing in the morning and ask if he could slap a fresh coat of paint on it. Then, he put down his guitar and asked me about my father. I told him what I had told Veronica earlier in the week; that my father had disappeared under unusual circumstances on a business trip when I was a few months old.

"I'm sorry about that." he said. *"We all need fathers. At least my father waited until I was 16 until he hit the road and started another family. But what I discovered was, I could have another*

family too. Maybe not my biological one, but a spiritual one. It's something called a 'Karass'. Kurt Vonnegut described a Karass as a group of people who inhabit your space in a very strong way. They might come and go, or they could be around for your entire life. If you are attuned to it you'll notice people seem to show up just when you need them the most. Like your friend Bob Robertson. Sure, he's a bit strange, but he showed up for a reason. You might not know what that reason is, but someday you might understand. Or not. That's the way life is. Full of mystery. Not knowing something can often be a beautiful thing. We need to accept the fact that we can't control everything because, more often than not, there's a different cosmic plan for us than the one that's in our heads. Which can be either terrifying or exciting, depending on how we choose to look at it. I don't know about you, but I wouldn't want it any other way."

On Saturday morning there was an all you can eat buffet in the main dining room at the Inn and they rarely asked for anyone's room number. Veronica and I met in the hotel lobby and pretended we were a couple when the maître d met escorted us to a table for two next to the windows. We had decided earlier that if anyone asked us for our room number we would be Thomas and Tess D'Urberville from Toledo, Ohio and that we were so in love we'd forgotten our room number. As we wolfed down eggs benedict and plates piled high with sausages and bacon we laughed about the machete Briny had found that almost ended up in my back.

Trying not to sound judgmental, I asked Veronica, "*When was the last time you ate?*"

"*Give me a break. I skipped dinner last night. Are you going to eat those sausages?*"

"*Nope. They're all yours. Here, take the English muffin. I'm not that hungry. I had steak with Mr. Robertson a few days ago and I'm still full.*"

"*Lucky you.*" she said in between bites. "*How did it go? Did you find out anything more about your father? Like what actually happened to him?*"

"*A little, but not much.*" I told her. "*He fell asleep before we got to that?*"

"*Well, at least that's a start. I'm sure you'll have plenty of time to talk this summer. After so much time has passed, it doesn't seem like he would have any reason to hide anything from you. Unless he's protecting your father, for some reason. You know you could always hire a private detective to try to find out what happened to him".*

"My mom already tried that. She didn't get anywhere. She knows something, and she told me she wanted to talk about it, but I'm not sure I really want to know. Either something bad happened to him or he left us because he didn't want to marry my mother and raise me. Either way it's bad news. All that really matters is he's gone and he's not coming back".

"You sure about the English muffin?" she said. *"Because if you're not going to eat it..."*

"It's all yours" I replied. *"Here, take the grape jelly too."*

"Thanks!" she said. *"You know, if we're going to continue to use the bus we need to get it repainted. You wouldn't believe the looks we got from people who thought we were transporting a bunch of eight-year old criminals."*

"I agree." I told her. *"I already mentioned it to Julian who said he'd contact someone he knows who works in maintenance. I'm thinking blue. It's my favorite color and the yellow of the tee shirts doesn't really work. It will look like a school bus, and bring up unpleasant memories."*

"Makes no difference to me" she said as she polished off the English muffin. *"As long as it doesn't say 'Pennsylvania Department of Corrections'."*

At the staff meeting on Monday morning Julian commended us for not allowing anyone to get hurt on our trip to the waterfall and told everyone he had disposed of the weapon Briny had found that I had left locked in his desk drawer at Camp Club. He also said that he had put in a call to Carl in maintenance about repainting the bus and Carl had told him they were short-staffed and booked solid until late September. So, Julian explained, we had two choices. We could continue to drive around looking like bunch of criminals or paint the bus ourselves.

While the campers were in Arts & Crafts, Veronica and I sat on a bench outside the former storage facility drinking lemonade and trying to decide what color the bus should be. After we were unable to agree on a color, Veronica came up with a great idea.

"Maybe we should let the kids decide? Have some kind of a contest? Of course the final decision would be up to us, but we can let them be part of the process".

"That's a great idea!" I said. *"Plus it gives us something different to do this week.*

As soon as they spilled out of Arts & Crafts, we announced the plan and immediately I could see their imaginations running wild as they came up with ideas. Trying to slow them down we told them to come up with as many ideas as they wanted and we would post them on the walls of the Arts & Crafts building on Friday and choose a winner.

The thought of decorating a bus was so engaging that enthusiasm for most of the other activities fell by the wayside that week. Tennis lessons were cancelled. The arrows at archery remained in their quivers. It was almost impossible to get a seat at the large paint spattered table in the middle of the Arts & Crafts building. Parents told us they couldn't get their kids to come to the dinner table because they were so busy sketching in their rooms. The Arts & Crafts teacher told us she hadn't seen anything like it during her 32 summers working at Camp Club.

Finally the big day arrived. There were so many submissions that we ran out of tape and had to raid the nurse's cabinet for rolls of surgical tape and eventually band aids in order to get all the drawings posted on the walls of Arts and Crafts. To make the selection process fair and transparent we made sure nobody's name was on the drawings and we gave each of the kids three gold stickers in the shape of stars to attach to their favorite designs. It was painful at times watching them trying to decide which drawings they should award their stars to and we didn't want to rush them so we gave them the entire day to decide. Some of them waited until just before their parents arrived to pick them up, but by 3:47 that afternoon we had a clear winner. It was a swirling psychedelic design like a poster from the 60's and Veronica and I were both thrilled when the artist turned out to be the meekest girl in the entire camp who hadn't excelled at anything all summer. I will never forget the look on everyone's face when we realized for the first time how much talent was inside little Charlene Klotz.

Before everyone went home someone shouted, *"It needs a name!"* and seconds later someone else replied. *"SS Groovy!"* There was no need to vote, the bus had been christened.

Julian had been spending a lot of nights out recently. Sometimes I heard him coming up the creaky stairs just before sunrise and sometimes he didn't come home at all. I never asked where he was and he never volunteered any information about where he had been. All I knew was he never missed a morning staff meeting and he always appeared to be well rested and ready to go. He'd already gone out that Friday night when Veronica came by with a bottle of red wine and some cheese and crackers.

"I wasn't doing anything, and I figured you probably weren't doing anything, so I thought I'd come over and we could not do anything together." she said.

"Sounds like a plan." I told her. *"I'll get a corkscrew and see if I can find some glasses. Unless you'd prefer to drink from the bottle. Which is fine with me."*

"I'd prefer glasses if you have them. They don't have to match. Dixie cups are fine. As long as they don't still have mouthwash in them."

I was able to locate two similar glasses in the kitchen, and after I rinsed them out and poured the wine, I went into Julian's room and put on an album by Van Morrison. When I got back, she asked where Julian was I told her I didn't know but I said he'd been going out a lot lately he probably wasn't coming home that night.

"Is he seeing somebody? Does he have a girlfriend? Or a boyfriend?" she asked.

"I really have no idea. We're just roommates. We don't talk about personal stuff."

After we finished the cheese and crackers, I told her that I wanted to propose a toast and she moved closer to me on the couch as we prepared to clink our glasses together.

"A toast to my first dinner party. And not being alone on Friday night.

After we toasted each other and sipped the wine, she looked up at me and gave me a small kiss on the lips. It seemed almost like a dare. As if she wanted to see what would happen. For a brief moment we both sat there staring at each other as Van Morrison sang *Moondance* in Julian's bedroom. Veronica was two years older than me, and obviously she was much more experienced in romantic relationships. Her kiss felt like a challenge that I couldn't refuse, so I turned toward her and kissed her back, just a little more passionately than she had kissed me. Not to be outdone, she responded with an even deeper kiss than I had ever experienced in my short life. After that, things progressed rapidly as we embraced each other and rolled around on the living room couch until, a short time later, we noticed Van Morrison had stopped singing *Into the Mystic* and the needle was skipping rhythmically at the end of Side 1.

"I'll be right back." I said as I tried to free my left arm from underneath her shoulders where it had become pinned down earlier in the evening and was now completely asleep.

"Take your time" she said. *"I need to use the bathroom. I'll be back in a Jiffy."*

As she made her way to the bathroom I heard her muttering to herself.

"Jiffy? Where did that come from, and what does that even mean?"

Julian didn't come home that night, which was a good thing because Veronica spent the night sleeping in my small twin bed on the third floor of Cottage 16 while I listened to her low rhythmic breathing and tried not to move fearing that any movement might wake her up. As she lay next to me, I couldn't believe all the incredible things that had happened to me in the few short weeks since my 18th birthday. On the heels of that thought, I began to wonder when my string of good luck might come to an end? When she woke up in a few hours was Veronica going to regret what had happened last night? Were the other counselors at the staff meeting going to recognize that something had changed between us over the weekend? Was this ever going to happen again, or was this going to be one night stand? Were we going to have to keep this a secret? Just before dawn, when the birds began to chirp outside my bedroom window, I tried to push these thoughts out of my head and enjoy the moment before she woke up.

Veronica slept to around 8:30 and I thought I saw her smile when she opened her eyes and saw me sitting in the wicker chair across from the bed.

"Hi" she said as she rubbed the sleep out of her eyes.

"Hi back" I replied. *"How are you feeling?"*

"I'm okay. A little hung over, but I'll survive. Nothing a good cup of coffee won't cure."

"I'd make you one, but all we have is Nescafe Instant coffee and it's decaffeinated."

"That's not going to cut it. Maybe you could get me something from the Inn, while I shower and get dressed?"

"Sure" I said. *"I'll be back in a Jiffy."*

As I got up to leave, she wrapped herself in the sheet like a toga and made her way down the hallway to the bathroom, and behind her back I noticed she gave me the finger.

Things were different after that night. It wasn't that there was no longer any mystery left about what it would feel like for us to be together. For me, it was the opposite. Veronica had allowed me to dance with some of her most intimate feelings and once inside her private world I realized there were so many more rooms that I wanted to explore. I wasn't sure if she felt the same way, but I couldn't help but notice, when other people were around, she seemed more distant than she had been before. I certainly didn't have to worry about people thinking we were having a relationship. If anything, it looked more like we were having an argument. Before we became lovers, when we were just friends, things seemed a lot less complicated.

The following week at Camp club was all about decorating the bus. After Veronica and I picked up paint colors from the local hardware store, I parked the bus in front of Camp Club and we spread out drop cloths and ladders that we had borrowed from maintenance. After we papered the windows, we gave the kids paint rollers to apply the primer coat and ate our lunch as we waited for it to dry. It was Veronica's idea to use a "paint by numbers" approach to get the design onto the bus. Moving around the bus on the ladders, Veronica outlined the swirling patterns with painters tape until at the end of the day we had what looked like a giant zebra. After everyone got picked up and went home, Veronica and I numbered each of the sections.

I hadn't gone shopping for groceries, and the refrigerator in the kitchen at Cottage 16 was empty except for some tofu, lentils and brown rice that Julian seemed to be living on, so I chose to ignore his advice and see what the employee dining room had to offer. It was on the second floor of a square building next to the employee parking lot and when I went inside I saw that it resembled a prison cafeteria, except perhaps a little nicer. There were three long steel tables in the center of the room surrounded by metal chairs and against the wall was a row of steam tables with what looked like Salisbury steak, green beans, mashed potatoes and carrots. There must have been a kitchen behind the door on the back wall, but you couldn't see it. As I was getting my dining card punched by a heavy set Hispanic man who appeared to be reading a dirty novel, I saw Q sitting by himself at the end of one of the long tables. After I loaded up my plate and poured myself a glass of milk, I walked over and asked if I could join him.

"Be my guest" he said. *"This table was reserved for a wedding party, but they cancelled at the last minute. Bride must have got cold feet. Sit wherever you like. Danny, if I remember correctly. So how are things going over at Club Fed?"*

"They're good" I said. *"Guess you heard about the bus?"*

"Yeah, well, it's hard to keep a secret around here. Too many people with too much time on their hands. Even the employees. They hear things, and good gossip around here is hard to come by. So anything that is the least bit interesting gets talked about. And embellished. Before you know it a tiny bit of 'he said, she said' becomes front page headline news. It's amazing how fascinated people are about other people's misfortunes. Helps them forget about their own."

He talked while I finished my dinner and we found each other to be good company. He told me he was concerned about some things happening behind the scenes in the accounting department, but said he was uncomfortable discussing anything in the employees cafeteria. When I thanked him for keeping things glued together, he replied.

"Scotch tape my friend. We ran out of glue a few months back. Look, I gotta go. But I'll tell you what. Thursday is payday around here and after we make payroll, Karen and I celebrate by going to Johnnie Diamonds for happy hour. It's right next door to Western Union where the employees cash their checks and send money to their relatives in South America. After that they take whatever is left over and go next door and get smashed. Why don't you join us? Draft beer is fifty cents and the wings are out of this world. Plus, they don't check ID's. See if you can make it. It's a blast. You'll understand why nothing ever gets done around here on Fridays.

It took an entire day for us to paint the bus, and it was difficult to tell if more paint had ended up on the campers or the bus. When we were finally done, Veronica removed the paper from the windows and carefully pulled off the painters tape leaving behind a web of white lines in between the swirling psychedelic patterns. Using a stencil Meredith from Arts & Crafts had painstakingly cut out, we spray painted SS GROOVY onto the front, back and sides of the bus in phosphorescent colors. After we christened her with a bottle of Orange Crush, I drove her back to the maintenance facility where we were greeted by cheering and a round of applause from the returning work crews.

Every summer there was a junior boys and girls excursion to Dorney Amusement Park in Allentown which wasn't far from where I grew up. I'd been there many times growing up and it was sprawling park with roller coasters, a Ferris wheel and several picnic areas where kids could easily wander away from the group and get lost. In keeping with the 60's theme of our bus, we decided to tie dye matching tee shirts so we would be able to identify our campers in a crowd. The good news was we were able to find most of the supplies in back of the Art & Crafts closet, so the only thing we needed do was pick up two dozen medium tee shirts at the Dollar Store. After the kids twisted the damp shirts into round balls held together with rubber bands, and applied the different color dye, we let the shirts soak overnight and rinsed them the following morning in the washing machine at the girls cottage across the street from Camp Club.

In case you've never been to Dorney Park, let me try to explain what it feels like to go. Like I said, it's a good-sized amusement park with seven roller coasters, one of which set the world record for having the longest drop on a wooden roller coaster of 151 vertical feet. There is also a scenic railway that takes you around the park past wooded picnic areas and a lake. When I was 6 years old I got lost in the park and a security guard brought me to a waiting area underneath the Thunderhawk roller coaster where I sat on a long wooden bench with several other kids my age with tears streaming down their bright red cheeks as they waited for their mothers to pick them up. Ever since then, I've had an intense fear of roller coasters. Not just a fear of riding on them, but also a fear of being near them. I didn't mention this to Veronica, who seemed to enjoy them immensely, but I knew it was something I was going to have to overcome at some point. I was just hoping that day was going to be off in the distant future.

All the kids in our group were over 42 inches tall, so technically they were allowed to go on almost every ride in the park. This was good news for them but bad news for me, because I quickly found out many of them still needed the reassurance of an "adult" sitting next to them on some of the more terrifying rides. After Veronica had gone on the Hurricane for the 6th time she told me it was my turn and I felt a lump in my throat and a queasy feeling in my stomach.

"No problem. I love roller coasters" I said trying to convince myself.

Thankfully Briny and I weren't in the front car, but I felt a surge of panic come over me when the attendant locked the bar in place across our laps so we wouldn't fall out. Then came the familiar "clack, clack, clack" as the car jerked away from the platform and we were pulled upwards into the sky at a ridiculous angle. As we climbed higher I felt my grip tighten on the cold metal bar that was pushed down across our laps and I started to notice spasms running across my back and shoulders. *"Breathe!"* I said trying to relax.

"What?" asked Briny. *"I can't hear you."*

"We…are having so much fun!"

The clacking sound made it almost impossible to talk as we climbed above the park and I looked down at the shrinking people below and out at the rolling hills surrounding the park. In the parking lot I saw the SS Groovy looking more like a toy bus than a real one. As soon as we reached the apex of the roller coaster, the clacking noise suddenly stopped and we heard the hook that had been attached to the chain that had been pulling us skyward disengage and the six cars rolled slowly forward toward the edge of a precipitous drop. After the first drop I told myself the worst was over and all I had to do was not tense up and try to relax. Even though the entire ride lasted a little more than 90 seconds, it felt like a lifetime to me. When we finally rolled to a stop at the boarding platform I felt a tremendous sense of accomplishment at having confronted one of my deepest fears, and not having anyone else know about it.

We ate lunch in the picnic grove and after that Veronica and I tried to keep track of the kids as they played arcade games beneath an enormous three-dimensional likeness of a clown named Alfundo who appeared to juggle giant colored balls over our heads. The name Alfundo, I later learned, came from a mash up of letters from Allentown Fun at Dorney Park. At any given time there were as many as thirteen Alfundos roaming around the grounds performing magic tricks and giving away tiny Alfundos to children in the park. Which brings me to my second confession. In addition to roller coasters, I am terrified of clowns and have always been deeply suspicious of Santa Claus. It's just the way my brain works. Anyone who wears a mask or too much makeup or pretends to be someone or something they're not has always made me very uncomfortable. So when Veronica bought an Alfundo mask for Halloween, because she thought it was cute, I was naturally horrified. Different strokes for different folks, I suppose.

After I dropped everyone off at camp club and parked the SS Groovy back behind the maintenance building, Veronica invited me over for dinner. Her roommate Kendra had been growing vegetables in a field behind the house since the beginning of summer and she had prepared an amazing salad with giant beefsteak tomatoes that had just become ripe.

"*It's the ugly ones you want. The ones with the long brown cracks in them*" she said as she slid her sharp knife through the dark red meat of the tomato. "*The ones at the store look great, but they taste like Styrofoam. No flavor at all. These are a real slice of heaven!*"

As we enjoyed Kendra's tomatoes, Veronica pulled a loaf of toasted garlic bread out of the oven and brought over a large bowl of steaming hot spaghetti topped with homemade tomato sauce and fresh basil from Kendra's garden. After Veronica and I washed the dishes and her roommates said goodnight, she asked me if I wanted to see her room. Since she was living in what was a girls dormitory, one of rules of the house was no men were allowed upstairs after 10:00. There wasn't anyone around to enforce it, but the girls liked their privacy and everyone pretty much abided by the rules. When I reminded her about this, she thought it over for a brief moment and dug into her purse and pulled out the Alfundo clown mask.

"*Here*" she said. "*Put this on and nobody will know you are a male.*"

"*You've got to be kidding*" I told her. "*I probably should have mentioned this earlier, but I'm absolutely terrified of clowns. And if Kendra, or one of your other roommates sees a clown coming up the back stairs at night I'm pretty sure she will have a heart attack.*"

"*Point well taken*", she said. "*We'll skip the clown mask. Just try not to make any noise*". Quietly, we tiptoed up the back staircase and slipped into her room. It was a small rectangular room like mine with a single gabled window that overlooked Camp Club. There was a lacrosse stick by the door and a pink

Teddy Bear on her bed. The only chair in the room was covered with clothes, so when she asked me to sit down I looked around and sat on the edge of her bed.

"Why didn't you tell me you were afraid of roller coasters? After you got off, you were as white as a ghost. They don't bother me. I would have sat next to Briny, if you'd told me."

"I guess I was embarrassed." I said. *"But I'm glad I did it. It kind of helped me get over some of my fears. The next time I do it, if there ever is a next time, I'll be better prepared."*

Any other fears that I should know about?" she said as she draped a red scarf over her bedside lamp giving her bedroom a warm, romantic glow. *"Are you afraid of the dark? Because if you are, we can always leave the light on?"*

"I'm fine with the light the way it is." I said as she leaned over and kissed me on the lips the way she had done the other night. For some reason Veronica was a lot more assertive and confident than she had been the first night we slept together. Maybe it was the excitement of all those roller coasters that day? I had to remind her several times to be quiet so she wouldn't wake up the girls down the hall. She told me where and how she wanted me to kiss her and what she wanted me to do and

her breaths quickened as I touched her in places I had never touched a woman before. As we tried to get comfortable in her small bed, she turned and rolled up on top of me and threw off the sheet allowing me to see her naked body and for us to look into each other's eyes as we made love in her small second floor bedroom. As we wrapped our arms around each other that night in her tiny bedroom everything that was going on around us seemed to melt away and disappear. All that mattered was the warmth of her body pressed up against mine, the silky softness of her hair and the sweet taste of her lips. When she shivered, I pulled her down comforter up over us and asked her if she was cold, but she told me she wasn't.

"*Just hold me*" she said, so I did. Not long after that we fell asleep in each other's arms. When I awoke, just before dawn, and tried to find my clothes in her darkened room, I noticed Alfundo, the creepy amusement park clown, had watched our every move from her dresser.

Two days later Veronica and I went on our first actual date. On the drive home from the amusement park we had passed a billboard announcing one of her favorite bands, Hall & Oates, was playing at the Allentown fairgrounds that weekend which wasn't far from where I grew up and when I called for tickets there were still plenty available. The Fairgrounds was nothing more than a grandstand and a stage with a large open field in between. General Admission got you inside the gates and then it was up to you to get as close to the stage as you felt comfortable.

We got there a half hour before the show started and after we each got a large beer and ate food on sticks we maneuvered our way to within ten feet of the stage. Backed by a six man band they opened the set with their hit song *Maneater* followed by *Kiss is on my list, Private Eyes, Rich Girl* and *Out of Touch.* Before that night, I hadn't realized they had so many hit songs that I knew all the words to. To conclude the main set, Daryl Hall played the grand piano and John Oates took over lead guitar for a long version of *Sara Smile* and I held Veronica tightly in my arms as she swayed back and forth to one of her favorite songs. It turned out to be a great concert and a well-behaved crowd and they closed with a six minute version of *You make my dreams come true,* which was exactly what I was thinking as I held Veronica in my arms but was too young and insecure to tell her. Anyway, thanks to Daryl Hall and John

Oates I didn't have to tell her what I was feeling because, at least in my own mind, they were expressing how I felt. We slept together again after the concert, although neither of us actually got much sleep.

After the last camper was picked up from Camp Club on Thursday afternoon, I borrowed a bike that someone had left behind the building and rode to Johnnie Diamonds to meet Q and his girlfriend. It was packed, just like he said, and I breezed past the bouncer who was leaning backwards on a bar stool just outside the front door. As soon as I got in, I ordered a "Jenny", which was short for *Genesee Cream Ale*, and looked around to see if I could locate Q. When I didn't see him in the front room, I made my way to the back porch where a bunch of heavily lubricated hotel employees were singing "*Sweet Home Alabama*". Once I pushed my way past them, I saw Q and his girlfriend at a high top in front of a plate of chicken wings, a bowl of nachos and a pitcher of draft beer. As soon as he saw me he stood up and waved me over.

"*You showed up!*" he shouted. "*We made payroll again, so we're celebrating! Say hello to my girlfriend Karen Kelly. Karen, this is the guy I told you about. Danny Barnes. He's keeping an eye on the kids down at Camp Club this summer, making sure they don't get into any trouble. I haven't heard of any problems so far, so he must being doing a good job."*

"So far so good" I said. *"The kids are great and pretty much up for anything. Keeping them busy isn't a problem. The hard part is telling them we can't do everything."*

"Tell me about it." said Karen. *"I spent almost every summer at Camp Club, and I was a CIT one year. Counselor in Training. It was fun, but my passion has always been cars. My dad owns a bunch of dealerships, so I asked him if I could help him out one summer and now I spend most of my time doing sales and marketing. Maybe you've seen our commercials on late night TV? The ones with the singing frog? That was my idea."*

Don't go broke,
or want to croak,
go to Jack Kelly Motors!

"You can laugh, but our sales go up 23% every time we run the commercials. It's pretty hard to forget seeing a singing frog wearing a tuxedo. Especially if he looks like my father."

When I asked them how they met she told me her father had sent her to the Inn to drop some sales materials for a dealer meeting and when she went to park she saw this really cool car.

"It was a '73 Pontiac Firebird with rally wheels in Brewster green, which was a 'one year only' color. I could tell by the sound of the engine it was a 455, not the standard 250 and it had a small Firebird on the front. They didn't make many of those, so I knew whoever was behind the wheel really appreciated cars. Then, this nerdy looking guy gets out of the car and asks me what I'm looking at. 'Your car', I said. 'You got a problem with that?' He said 'No'. So I ask what the compression is and without hesitating he tells me it's '8.4 to one'. So I knew this was a car guy. Beautiful set of wheels, I told him. Really. Then he asks for my number and says he'll take me for a ride sometime. Maybe even let me drive, as long as I was old enough? After I told him I'd been driving since I was 14 and I was twenty three, I gave him my number and a few days later he called and picked me up at the dealership. My father wasn't too keen on us dating since he was so much older than me, but they're friends now. Anyway, what all this told me was this guy was for real. Not just some loser who

buys a fancy car to impress girls. Funny, huh? No offense Q, but that was exactly what happened.

After we finished the plate of wings and had two more pitchers of beer the conversation circled back to what had been bothering Q.

"I just can't figure it out." he said. *"The numbers are the numbers. They should add up, but they don't. Overhead and expenses are down and revenue is up, but we can't seem to get out of the red. I brought it up with Karen's dad, but he's got too much on his plate running the dealerships. I have no idea what Szabo is up to but he keeps telling me not to worry about it but there have been a lot of late night meetings with some pretty shady characters.*

Who's Szabo?" I asked.

"The general manager. You're not paying attention. The guy who can't find the men's room, remember? I tried to introduce you but he skulked away. Creepy dude who grew up in Atlantic City. He worked at the Sands Hotel, where Sinatra used to sing. Look, I'm not saying he's in the mob, but something deep inside my gut tells me he's somehow connected."

I had no idea why Q was telling me any of this, but I guess it was because nobody else would listen to him and he felt the need to blow off some steam. He probably figured I was just a kid, a nobody from nowhere, so what was the harm in telling me what was keeping him up at night. After we split the bill three ways, I paid my share and thanked Q for inviting me and told Karen if I ever made enough money to be able to buy a car, the first place I would go would be Jack Kelly Motors. She laughed and said she would take good care of me and I believed her, so I knew she must have been a pretty good salesperson like her father.

Like most places in America, the fourth of July was a pretty big deal at Buck Hill and Q invited me to join him for a barbeque at the Kelly's house which was on a hill overlooking the golf course where the fireworks were being set off that evening. When I told him I planned to do something with Veronica he told me to bring her along, so I accepted. When we arrived I was pleasantly surprised to see Bob Robertson holding court with some of his golf cronies next to the bar. As soon as he was finished telling one of his notoriously off color jokes, I walked up and introduced him to Veronica.

"What a lovely young lady!" he said as he admired the provocative dress she had chosen to wear to the barbeque. *"I hope you didn't overhear the punchline to that last joke. And if you did, I hope you will be able to forgive me. What's a nice girl like you doing in a place like this?"*

"I'm a camp counselor, just like Danny." she told him. *"We're kind of paired up. I want to thank you for bringing him here. He's doing a really good job."*

"Well of course he is." said Bob. *"He takes after his father who happened to be a very good friend of mine and was a very responsible person. I miss him like a brother, but it brings me joy to have Danny here this summer. How do you know Jack and Diane? I had to buy three cars before I got invited to their Fourth of July party, and you've only been here a few weeks."*

Before I could answer, Karen came over and told Bob she had invited us and reminded him that his lease was up for renewal in August but suggested he wait until September, when the new models came in, before making a decision.

"Quite a salesperson, that one." he said. *"Takes after her father who could sell ice to an Eskimo. Speaking of ice, I need to refresh my drink. These days everyone seems to be drinking*

Harvey Wallbangers, but I'm more of a traditionalist. Care to slip into a nice dry martini?"

After we raised our glasses to thank Thomas Jefferson for writing the Declaration of Independence, and cursed the King of England, we loaded up our plates with food that was spread out across a large picnic table in the Kelly's back yard. The hamburgers were cooked perfectly and placed on large soft buns next to large colorful bowls of potato salad and fresh coleslaw. The corn on the cob had been picked that morning and the small, white kernels were so sweet and delicious that we didn't need to coat them with butter. But we did anyway. And at the far end of the table were rows of bright red triangular wedges of watermelon and a large platter of warm chewy fudge brownies that had just come from the oven.

After we were finished eating, we sat on a blanket on the hill behind the Kelly's cottage and looked down over the long green expanse of the 17th fairway where we could see a group of men wearing jumpsuits waiting for it to become dark enough to start the fireworks display.

Finally we heard something go THUMP and then WHOOSH as the first firework rose up into the sky leaving behind a trail of glittering sparks. Then BOOM, it exploded over our heads with a shower of extraordinary particles of light. As soon as it disappeared we heard THUMP, THUMP, THUMP as three more fireworks shot up into the sky and burst into brilliant blossoms of red, white and blue. After that the explosions kept coming and didn't stop until the sky was saturated with larger and larger blooms of incandescent color and the air smelled of sulfur.

By the middle of July the kids were getting bored doing the same old things week after week and Veronica and I were having a hard time coming up with new ideas. As a last resort, I proposed a trip an Army-Navy surplus store a few towns away that I thought might be worth a visit. The kids liked the idea, so the next day we piled into the SS Groovy and drove to East Stroudsburg to see what the store had to offer. Inside were mannequins dressed like soldiers from both world wars and a few from the Civil War Era for people who enjoyed reenactments, which were quite popular in Pennsylvania. In one corner was a Japanese machine gun nest complete with sandbags and what looked like boxes of live ammunition. There were walls of bayonets and tactical knives and shelves stacked high with every kind of helmet imaginable from German Pickelhaubes with points on top to modern SWAT team helmets.

In the center of the store were racks of moldy smelling camouflage uniforms with the soldiers names still stitched over the pocket. Gas masks, walkie-talkies and a few things that looked like bombs but might have been torpedoes, hung from the ceiling looking like they were about to drop on our heads. A few of the kids bought some old uniforms and everyone pitched in to buy a set of World War II walkie-talkies used by the Signal Corps. Before the kids counted out their hard-earned allowances, Veronica made the owner prove to us that they still worked. They looked like large bricks and as I carried one out to the parking lot to try to determine its range I saw that it was made by Galvin manufacturing, which I later learned took the words Motor and Victrola and mashed them together to become Motorola

Naturally, the kids were eager to try out their new / old camouflage uniforms, so instead of going directly back to Camp Club we parked the bus in the woods next to the golf course and decided to have a golf ball hunt. It was girls against boys and the only rules were you could not get caught, or even be seen, by anyone on the golf course. According to the bylaws, children of members were not permitted anywhere on the golf course unless they were accompanied by an adult who was also a member. There were no exceptions. One of the things Julian had been very clear about was that the golf course was strictly off limits. I knew it was risky, so I told the kids they would only have 45 minutes to collect as many golf balls as they could find.

"Ready, set, go!" said Veronica as the kids disappeared into the woods. After they left, Veronica and I went off in different directions to make sure everyone stayed off the golf course. The time passed quickly, and after 45 minutes was up Veronica blew her whistle three times signaling the game was over and everyone needed to return to the bus. When we counted the golf balls it was dead even. Both teams had found 37 golf balls and nobody was happy about things ending in a tie. After considerable debate, Veronica and I decided to give them 15 more minutes to see if they could come up with a winner.

The girls, we later learned, were much more serious about winning than the boys and Alison, their self-appointed leader, decided it was time to tilt the playing field in their favor.

"No more hiding in the woods." she instructed her eager platoon. *"Penelope will be positioned on the ridge with the binoculars. Take the walkie-talkie. When you see a ball in the air, I want you to tell Dana exactly where it lands. Do you understand? We're moving onto the golf course, but we won't be seen. Grab some branches. Position yourselves near the bunkers. That's where all the balls go. I know because my father plays golf. Now move out!"*

A few minutes later, I heard Penelope's voice coming in loud and clear on the walkie-talkie. *"Whiskey, tango, foxtrot, incoming! Bravo company, storm the beach!"*

"Roger that" came the response. *"Boots are on the move!"*

As the golfers made their way down the fairway, I heard one of them ask his caddy, *"What on earth is that shrub doing in front the bunker!? You wouldn't see that at Augusta."*

Puzzled, his caddy replied, *"I have no idea, Mr. Knight. Wasn't there yesterday"*.

Cautiously the older gentleman addressed the ball, took a swing and launched it directly into the bush in front of the bunker. After he replaced his divot and jammed his club forcefully back into his golf bag, he looked up and saw that the bush and his ball were no longer there.

"Great jumping Jehoshaphat!" he said to his astonished caddy. *"If you want to continue working here, you're going to tell me right now exactly what the hell is going on!"*

After giving it some thought, I heard his caddy say, *"Squirrels. They've been a real nuisance this year. No nuts, sir. Good news is you get a free drop."*

Everyone hit their drive perfectly on the next hole which was a par five dog leg right. However, nobody, not even the caddies, seemed to notice that a small grouping of trees had appeared on the turn moments earlier. After the allotted time had expired, each of the four golfers was forced to declare his ball lost and hit a provisional. Many years later, while sitting around reminiscing, it was something they still talked about.

After the foursome finished putting out, Veronica blew her whistle three more times signaling for the campers to return to the bus so we could once again count the golf balls. This time, the girls won decisively and I awarded them a "trophy" that I had found wrapped around a tree next to the 7th green. It was mangled putter that looked like a snake about to strike.

They loved it, and Veronica's girls put on a celebratory dance similar to what happens after a football team scores the winning touchdown.

On the drive home that afternoon, the campers sang a song their parents, and some of their grandparents, had sung when they were at Camp Club.

Camp club is my favorite place
There we have rattlesnakes
Poison oak between our toes
Little gnats up our nose
The last time I was there
I even saw a grizzly bear
Camp club is my favorite place.

After the last camper was picked up, Veronica told me she thought we should go on a more formal date. "*Something fun. just the two us. What should it be?*" After I proposed hustling pool at *Billie's*, a popular lesbian biker bar, Veronica suggested we push Billie's back to our second or third date and start with dinner at her favorite Italian restaurant, *Maccioni's.*

"Sounds great" I told her. *"I have another idea that might be fun. Have you ever been to the Pocono Playhouse? I hear they have some pretty good shows there."* When she said she'd never been, but had always wanted to go, we decided I would look into getting tickets to a play and when we knew what day we were going, she would make a dinner reservation.

What had sparked the idea of going to the Pocono Playhouse was the long standing tradition at Buck Hill of Camp Club putting on a play first week of August. It was up to the senior boys and girls counselors to pick the play and Garrett and Molly had chosen the Wizard of Oz. The costumes weren't too difficult to figure out. All we needed was some straw, aluminum foil and a fur coat for three main characters. Add to that a pair of red pumps, some glitter and lots of green paint. The smaller kids could be munchkins, Veronica had agreed to be Almira Gulch who became the Wicked Witch of the West and I played Chester Marvel, the traveling fortune teller who became the Great and Powerful Oz. There were a few songs that everybody could learn and sing and it had a happy ending. The hard part was trying to keep it under an hour, including set changes, so we left out some scary scenes that we hoped nobody would miss.

On Wednesday, after play practice, I waited around for Briny's mother to pick him up but after 45 minutes she still hadn't showed up. She played tennis on Tuesdays and sometimes she showed up five or ten minutes late and apologized profusely. But every other day her BMW was waiting in the lineup with the other cars just before 4:00. I tried to find Julian to ask him to call the house, which was the usual protocol, but he wasn't around. Finally, I told Briny to grab his backpack and told him I would walk him home. It wasn't far and play practice seemed to be mostly sitting around waiting to deliver your lines. We were both still in costume when I walked him home. I was wearing an old tuxedo and Briny, who had been picked to play the Cowardly Lion, was wearing tan pajamas with a tail. As we walked, I asked him if his father was going to come to see the play on Friday. That way I would have a chance to meet him. I hadn't seen his father all summer, but I assumed he came up for weekends.

"My dad said he would try to come" Briny told me. *"He hasn't been here much. Only once. He said he was sorry. He has to work almost every weekend."*

When I asked Briny what his father did for a living, he hesitated for a moment.

"He's a persecutor" he said. *"He puts bad people in jail. There must be lots of bad people because my dad is very busy. My mom wants him to get a different job. So he can spend more time with us. But he says he loves his job. That makes her sad."*

Deciding to change the subject, I asked him what he liked to do in his free time.

"I collect stuff" he told me. *"Rocks, baseball cards, pennies. Pennies are easy to collect. Nobody even cares about a penny. Ask someone for a penny and they'll say, 'Here, take them all'. People think pennies aren't good for anything, just making change and taking up space in your pocket. But they are wrong. There are millions of valuable pennies out there that are still in circulation. Because nobody notices them. At Lewis's grocery store last week, the man at the cash register gave my mom a 1939 Lincoln Wheat penny! Guess how much it's worth?"*

"I really have no idea?" I said. *Two dollars?"*

"Five! I have a book that tells you exactly how much every penny is worth. And I have a penny for almost every year since

1909, except for a few years. I can show you my collection sometime, If you're interested?

"I'd like that" I said. *Tell me which ones you're missing and I'll keep a lookout for them."* Briny liked that idea, and before we knew it we had arrived at their cottage. His mother's dark green BMW was parked in the driveway, so I assumed she must be home. After we opened the front door and walked in, Briny dropped his backpack on the floor in the foyer and I heard the sound of voices coming from the kitchen. As we turned the corner I saw Mrs. Bell leaning back against the kitchen counter wearing a loose fitting floral print dress and holding a large glass of red wine. She was barefoot and noticeably startled when she saw Briny wearing his Cowardly Lion outfit and me dressed in a tuxedo. And why wouldn't she be? I'd never been to her house and I was sure I looked ridiculous wearing someone else's grandfather's old tuxedo. But as we stepped into their kitchen, I realized there was another reason she was uncomfortable. Sitting at their breakfast table, wearing a light blue chenille bathrobe, was Julian Snow. At first, the four of us just stared at each other. Nobody said a word until she forgot that she was

holding a wine glass and it fell from her hand and shattered into a million pieces on the limestone floor.

"Briny!" she shouted out. *"What are you doing home? What time is it? Are you okay?*

Trying to calm her down, I said *"Everything's fine Mrs. Bell. It was getting late, so when you didn't show up, after play practice, I walked Briny home."*

"Thank you!" she said exhaling deeply clutching her hands to her chest. *"I thought today was the 'long day', when practice was going until 7:00? But I must have made a mistake. Julian came by with some things Briny left at Camp Club. I'm so sorry, Briny"*.

Julian just sat there looking perfectly calm and relaxed. As if it was perfectly normal for him to be sitting in the Bell's kitchen on a Thursday afternoon in the middle of a sea of broken glass on what looked like a slaughterhouse floor wearing a baby blue chenille bathrobe talking to the Cowardly Lion and the Great and Powerful Oz.

"How was play practice? Julian asked Briny who was temporarily unable to speak.

"It was fine" I said. *"The kids were exhausted, so we decided to cut it short. We tried to call all the parents, but not everyone answered their phone. We tried several times, Mrs. Bell. But I guess you must have been busy."*

"Sometimes our phone doesn't work" she said. *"I've been meaning to have it looked at, but I haven't had time. I guess I'd better get around to getting it fixed."*

When she started to walk barefoot through the glass, Julian told her not to move.

"Libby, stay where you are. Tell me where I can find a mop so we can get this cleaned up before someone gets hurt."

"There's a broom and a dust pan in the closet" she told him. *"If you can make me a path, I'll put on my sandals and sweep up the glass. It's something Briny and I have been working on, right? Taking responsibility for things. Cleaning up after ourselves. Not having someone else clean up things after we've make a mess of them. Which I've obviously done."*

When she got down on her hands and knees and began to scrub the kitchen floor, I asked Briny if he wanted to show me his penny collection. We were both glad to go upstairs and as I sat on his bed admiring the folders full of pennies he had collected, I heard her sobbing downstairs and Julian doing his best to comfort her.

Thankfully, by the time we came down, Julian had removed the blue bathrobe and was wearing the clothes he usually wore to Camp Club. As we walked back to Cottage 16 that night there were so many things I wanted to ask Julian but didn't know where to start. Like what was going on between the two of them and why on earth was he wearing that ridiculous bathrobe? Instead, we walked in silence the entire way home and after we ascended the dark staircase to the third floor of Cottage 16, he disappeared into his bedroom and closed the door.

At the fourth of July picnic at the Kelly's house, Q and I had talked about how much he enjoyed hiking and being in the wilderness. I never would have guessed that he would be an outdoors type, but apparently he was. During summers in college he had hiked most of the Appalachian Trail which begins in Mount Katahdin, Maine and ends up somewhere in Georgia. Or vice versa, depending on which direction you choose. It's more than 2,000 miles long, so I guessed he couldn't possibly have done the whole thing, but quite a few people do. From what he told me, he had hiked some of the more interesting sections of the trail and was planning to complete the other, less interesting parts at a later date. Only a few hundred people each year accomplish what's called a "thru-hike" by completing the entire trail in one season. And a few crazies do what's called a "yo-yo" by turning around at the end of their "thru-hike" to complete the trail hiking back in the opposite direction.

I must have had more to drink that I probably should have at the Kelly's Fourth of July barbeque, because apparently I had enthusiastically agreed to go on a hike with Q and Karen that weekend. So when Karen came up the stairs of cottage 16 early Saturday morning, and awakened Veronica and me, I had to pretend we had merely overslept. Neither of us had hiking boots or equipment, so after we brushed our teeth and washed our faces we followed Karen back down the stairs and got into the backseat of Q's waiting car.

We didn't have time for breakfast, so you can imagine how happy we were when Q handed us each a steaming hot cup of coffee and a bag of freshly made donuts.

"Where did you get these?" I asked after I took a bite of the donut that had a crisp outer coating and was warm inside and covered with a light dusting of granulated sugar.

"There's a shop near my apartment that makes them fresh every day. You have to get there early, because there's a line out the door. Best breakfast burritos this side of Mexico and their coffee's not bad either" he told me.

It took us about an hour to drive to the trailhead where we parked next to a river and a large camper van. It was warm and muddy when we started out and everyone had to peel off clothes as we walked through the heavily pine scented forest, but as the trail got steeper, and we gained elevation, the air began to get cooler. There were a few places on the trail that were quite challenging and Q, who was an experienced climber, pointed out which root or branch was safe to grab onto so we could pull ourselves up several rocky escarpments.

After an hour and a half, we found ourselves above the tree line following piles of rocks that Q told us were 'cairns' and indicated the path we needed to follow to get to the top. He told us not to disturb them because animals and insects make their homes inside them, to hide from predators, and if we moved the rocks it would be like leaving the front door open.

Just below the summit, we left the marked trail and had to traverse a narrow ledge and lean into the side of the mountain to keep from falling several hundred feet into a deep ravine. Nobody mentioned this at the beginning of the hike, but once we started there was no turning back, so I reminded myself not to look down as we sidestepped across the ledge searching for cracks in the stone face that we could wedge our fingers into.

When we finally got to the other side, everyone including Q, breathed a sigh of relief and he promised that we would stick to the marked trail on the way back down.

On top of the mountain, we found a half circle of boulders that sheltered us from the wind as we wolfed down roast beef sandwiches and drank chocolate milk that Karen brought. While we rested our aching legs, we looked down at the lush green forests and strings of lakes and rivers that surrounded us on all sides like a giant multi-hued deep shag carpet.

We made it down the mountain in half the time it took for us to climb up, and our legs started to cramp in new places, totally different from the aches and pains we'd experienced on the way up. For me, it was just above the knee cap that began to feel “wobbly”. It didn’t help that we hadn’t brought nearly enough water and everyone was completely dehydrated.

The first stop on the way home was a gas station where we bought jugs of Gatorade and bags of potato chips to replenish our electrolytes and all the salt that we’d lost on the hike. Not exactly backpacker food but what was available at the gas station and what we were craving.

On the drive home I could tell that something was bothering Q and I had a pretty good idea it was what was happening in the accounting office. He liked his job, but I was pretty sure he could find another one if push came to shove. A few people in his department had left, and from the way he described it to me, he felt like he was watching rats leaving a sinking ship. It was his opinion, however, that the ship wasn’t just being abandoned, it was being scuttled.

After Q dropped us off, Veronica and I thanked him for everything he had done for us that day and he mentioned he was going to stop by the office on the way home to pick up a few things he wanted to work on over the weekend. Since it was Saturday, he had his choice of any parking spot in the employee parking lot, so just for fun, he took the one reserved for the GM. There was no way a guy like that would be working on a Saturday night. After he locked his car, he took the staff stairs up to the accounting office, rather than cut through the hotel lobby, which was discouraged. When he got to the entrance to the office he was surprised to see that the door was unlocked and had been left open. Maybe somebody had forgotten to lock up? Or perhaps the cleaning people? But then why were the lights off? As he moved inside and began to feel his way around the wall for the light switch he though he heard someone moving around in the darkness.

"Hello?" he called out into the darkness. *"Anyone here?"* When he didn't get a reply, he decided to let the silence know what was going on. "*If anyone is here, I want you to know that it's me, Q. I just need to pick up a few things from my desk. So I'm going to turn on the lights, and I don't want to startle you. Unless you are a raccoon. Because I know raccoons don't like light. So on the count of three I'm going to turn on the lights. One, two...*

Before he could say "three", he heard something move in the darkness and was blinded by a sudden flash of light. The last thing he remembered, after he felt a heavy blow to the back of his neck, was the floor rising up toward his face just before he lost consciousness.

When he woke up six hours later, the lights in the office were on and except for some scattered papers on the floor, things looked pretty much normal. Whoever had been in the office that night had left in a hurry, because the door was open and the Swingline stapler that had been used as a weapon was still laying on the floor next to his throbbing head. Remarkably, there was no blood, but a large round bump had already appeared at the base of his skull.

Steadying himself on the messy desks as he stumbled across the large open office, he made his way to the refrigerator in the kitchen where he found a bag of frozen vegetables to press against the goose egg above his neck. He was extremely fortunate the blow had not been two inches lower, where it would have struck one of seven vertebras that are part of the cervical spine which could have left him paralyzed.

Unable to remember why he came to the office in the first place, he reached down in pain to pick up his set of keys, flicked off the lights, locked the door and drove himself home.

After the hike, Veronica had spent the night at her place claiming she needed to get a good night's rest and that wasn't going to happen if we shared my small bed at Cottage 16. We had been together a lot lately, and to be perfectly honest I didn't mind having a night to myself. On Sunday mornings, her typical routine was to get up early and go for a run. Sometimes she would stop by after her run and we would have coffee on the balcony of Cottage 16. We'd both been so exhausted after the hike we hadn't made any plans to get together, so I was pleasantly surprised when I saw her jogging up the loose stone driveway.

"Howdy stranger" she shouted, trying to catch her breath. *"Mind if I come up?"*

"Door's open" I called down to her. *"Your timing could be perfect."*

When she came up the stairs she saw Julian sitting cross legged in the center of the room surrounded by what looked like a small combustion engine.

"I give up Julian. What is it?" she said looking at the metal parts that were scattered all over the floor. *"Some kind of boiler?"*

"You are not wrong" said Julian without looking up. *"It's an espresso machine. Or at least it will be, if I can figure out how to get it to work. And I think we're getting close."*

While we we're on our hike, Julian had gone to a flea market in Dingmans Ferry where he found an exquisite copper and brass *Elektra Belle Epoque commercial espresso machine*. Even if he wasn't able to get it to work, it would have made a fine looking piece of sculpture.

Not sure why there were so many leftover parts, Julian took a deep breath and decided there was nothing left to do except plug her in and see if she worked. After we walked the heavy machine over to the wall, Julian grabbed the frayed plug and handed it to Veronica.

"Please, if you wouldn't mind. I believe we have a much greater chance of success if she is plugged in by a beautiful woman, such as yourself."

When I saw a concerned look on her face, I went to the kitchen and came back with an ancient-looking fire extinguisher and said, *"Got your back"* trying to sound reassuring.

"If this thing catches on fire, you need to put me out first. Do you understand? And not just my back. My front and my sides and whatever else is burning. Okay?"

"Of course" I said as I looked for a gauge or a date on the cylinder that might indicate it wasn't already empty and still worked, but I couldn't find anything. As I look back on that day, it probably didn't inspire confidence when she watched me put my finger inside the rusty metal ring that was there to prevent the antique fire extinguisher from going off accidentally.

When she jammed the plug into the wall socket, nothing happened at first, so I reached down and gave it a jiggle. Instantly, a blue spark shot out of the switch plate and knocked me backwards causing me to drop the extinguisher on my right foot. As I reached down to massage my injured toes, we heard a whirring noise, and shortly after that, small jets of steam started to pour out of several holes that had been drilled in the front and sides of the machine.

"It's working!" shouted Julian, reminding me of Dr. Frankenstein standing over the body of his newly resurrected creation. Each of the steaming holes, some of which were beginning to whistle, was a different size which helped us

figure out which part went into which hole like a giant three dimensional jigsaw puzzle. Eventually, the only place where steam was coming from was just above the Portafilter, where the coffee grounds went, and after Julian finished turning a round wooden knob on the front of the machine, the machine was finally silent.

"We need more water!" said Julian. *"And grab that bag of coffee from my room."*

We heard a tremendous hissing sound when Julian poured the water into the large reservoir in the back of the machine. After he latched the lid on the reservoir, he measured out three spoonful's of rich, dark ground coffee, pressed them into the Portafilter and attached it securely with a twist of his wrist to the overhanging nozzle of the machine where it fit perfectly.

A man of many hidden talents, Julian seemed to know exactly how to moderate the temperature and pressure of the machine as he filled an antique Italian coffee cup that he had purchased with the machine at the flea market with the dark, earthy brew that dripped from two small holes in the bottom of the wooden handled Portafilter. Unlike the coffee I would get from a coffee shop or brew at home, Julian's coffee had a thick creamy head like you might see on a pint of Guinness. After Veronica took a sip, she and rolled her eyes in amazement.

"Bravo Julian!" she said. *"Or should I say, Bravissimo!"*

"Both are technically correct." He replied. *"But I would say Bellissima! Because she is so beautiful. It's not the conductor who deserves the praise, it's the musicians who play the music."*

After we finished our coffee and unplugged the machine, Julian excused himself and went back to his room to take to shower. Once we were alone, Veronica suddenly got quiet and told me there was something we needed to talk about.

"There is something I need to tell you. And just to give you fair warning, you're not going to be very happy with me after I tell you. Because I haven't been completely honest with you. So I want to apologize beforehand. Before we met, I was seeing someone. And we didn't break up, so technically, I guess I'm still seeing someone. He doesn't know about you. And I didn't want to tell you about him because I wasn't sure what was happening between us. Until recently. And then it was kind of too late. So what I'm trying to say is, I kind of still have a boyfriend. And he called last night and told me he wants to come visit me. This weekend. When we were supposed to go on our date. Which

means I can't go. And there is a chance that you might meet him. And if that happens, it would be better for everyone if you didn't say anything about 'us'. Assuming there still is an 'us'. Which I completely understand there might not be, after this conversation. I just want to be completely honest with you. Even though it's a little late in the game. Not that love is a game. I didn't mean it that way. I take relationships very seriously. I've been hurt far too many times. But I can certainly understand how you might be feeling right now. And I'm really sorry. I wasn't expecting to meet someone like you. And the past few weeks have been very confusing for me. But I'm looking forward to sorting things out. And I hope you can be a little patient with me. And that no matter what happens, that we can still be friends".

When she was done, I felt like I'd been hit in the stomach with a cannon ball. All the air seemed to have gone out of my lungs and I felt like I was about to pass out. Strangely, the only word that would come out of my mouth was *"Okay"*. For the first time in my life, I knew what it felt like to be speechless. After that she took a breath, exhaled deeply, got up and walked out.

After he finished showering, Julian came back into the room wearing a towel and said *"Dude. Did I just hear what*

I think I heard? That she wants to 'still be friends'? Five most hurtful words in the English language. Please brother, tell me it isn't so?"

After I told Julian what Veronica had said, I decided to go for a run myself. I had hoped that things would start to get better from that point on, but they only got worse. For some reason, I decided to take a shortcut through the lobby of the hotel to my usual running route which began on a wooded path behind Camp Club. After I came down the stairs into the main reception area I somehow got tangled up in the leashes of three yapping dogs and ended up sprawled on the floor of the lobby while one of the dogs urinated on my leg.

"*Young man, I am so sorry*" said the owner, a woman in her mid-fifties. "*We probably should have stopped on the way to pee-diddle. Sorry about the strong smell. Winkie's diabetic.*"

Things were noticeably different between Veronica and me at the Monday morning staff meeting after she confessed that she already had a boyfriend. As I sat on the picnic table that day, unable to listen to what Julian was telling us about the week ahead, I racked my brain trying to remember if she had ever even hinted at having a boyfriend. We had shared a lot of secrets, talked about past loves, but nothing about him had ever come up. There were no pictures of him in her bedroom. No letters. No postcards. No "*While You Were Out*" notices. I was amazed at how well she had been able to keep him a secret from me, and I assumed, keep me a secret from him. They say 'love is blind', but you can't see what people don't show you.

One of the highlights of summer at Camp Club was the annual junior boys and junior girls camping trip to Metzger's Farm. Even though it was only a few miles away from Buck Hill Falls, it was world's away from the day to day activities of Camp Club. The farm was on the edge of 140 acres of dense forest and several small lakes and was a popular destination for bird watchers in the summer and hunters in the fall.

During the Great Depression a family from New York City had moved there and tried their hand at apple farming and raising sheep. However, similar to the investment business, they failed miserably. After six years, and three of the coldest winters in memory, they packed up and moved to New Hope, Pennsylvania where they lived on the third floor of a boarding house with their cousins who had found themselves in similar circumstances.

Everyone, that is, except for the patriarch, Winslow Evans Metzger who was convinced things would improve. Unfortunately, he was wrong. After his horse died, he no longer went to church on Sundays and earned a reputation of being an ornery hermit. Several years shy of his fortieth birthday, a young boy showed up on the farm and was seen working out in fields. One morning when a woman and a man from the local school district showed up unannounced to inquire why the boy wasn't in school, they discovered that he was unable or unwilling to speak.

Rumors circulated that Winslow Evans Metzger had fathered the child with a young woman who visited the farm once a week to purchase eggs while her husband was serving his country on the shores of Sicily. Many years later, after old man Metzger died, the boy disappeared and the Inn was granted a 99 year lease on the property in hopes of extending the holiday season by turning the hill into a ski slope and, but the plan never came to fruition.

I overslept the morning of the overnight and missed the staff meeting completely. When Julian saw me sleepily loading the camping gear and sleeping bags onto the bus he didn't say anything because he knew I was having trouble getting to sleep after Veronica dumped me. As Veronica and I circled each other counting backpacks and making sure we had all the supplies that we needed, I noticed she was unable to make eye contact. Finally, in an effort to make the situation easier on everyone, I cornered her and asked how she was doing.

"I'm fine" she said. *"And you?"*

"I'm okay. Having trouble sleeping, but other than that, I'm hanging in there."

"Good" she said. *"Then you're ready for the overnight, because nobody sleeps."*

After we loaded the last few boxes of food onto the bus, Veronica assembled the troops and we had a roll call to make sure nobody was missing. Before we left, Julian came by to wish us good luck and handed me the key to the gate which blocked the entrance to the campsite.

"Adios Amigos" he said as we drove off.

I drove North on Route 191 for about three miles and took a sharp left onto Metzger's Farm road before stopping in front a padlocked gate surrounded by No Trespassing signs. To the right of the gate, about 110 yards in front of us, was what remained of the farmhouse that must have belonged to the Metzger family surrounded by the rusting skeleton of a John Deere tractor and some farm equipment. After Veronica unlocked the gate, I put the bus in low gear and drove up the hill to the campsite where we unpacked and set up two separate camps.

Veronica decided the girls tents would be on the left side of the campground, closer to the bus, while the boys would be off to the right next to a clearing by the edge of the woods. In between the two camps was a circle of rocks where the kids could sit around a campfire.

We weren't exactly roughing it, because dinner that night was a delicious beef stew that had been prepared by the head chef at the Inn and all I had to do was be careful not to let the tremendous pot fall over while it was heating on the campfire. Nothing like a one pot meal.

After we cleaned up, the kids went back to their tents to get their flashlights and by the time everyone got back the flames of the campfire were reaching high into the night sky. As was the tradition of the overnight, we sang a few familiar Camp Club songs that had been sung by generations and ended with our own version of *Country Road* by John Denver.

Almost heaven, Pennsylvania
Pocono Mountains, long and winding rivers
Life is old here, older than the trees
Younger than the mountains, growin' like a breeze
Country roads, take me home
To the place I belong
Pennsylvania, mountain mama
Take me home, country roads

Another time honored tradition of the junior boys and girls overnight was the ghost story and it had fallen on my shoulders to deliver it that night. After we had finished making s'mores, I let the campfire die down before I started telling the story I had made up while Veronica and I were cleaning up after dinner.

"It was a dark and stormy night, exactly fifty years ago, when a young couple was driving to the Inn where the boy was

planning to ask his girlfriend to marry him. He had finally saved up enough money to buy a ring and had it safely tucked away in his coat pocket when a deer ran in front of the car causing him to swerve off the where the car hit a rock and got a flat tire. Unfortunately, when he got out of the car and stepped out into the rainy night to look for the spare tire, he noticed it was gone. Wondering what to do, he looked up Metzger's Farm road and saw a light on in the farmhouse at the base of this hill. Taking off his coat he wrapped it around his girlfriend and the two of them walked slowly up the long dirt road in the pouring rain to see if they could use the phone to call for help. When they knocked on the door, an old man answered and told them he didn't have a telephone, but they were welcome to spend the night and the next day he would find someone to help them repair the flat tire. After the man's son brought them each a bowl of hot soup they went to sleep in the guest bedroom where the young man hid the engagement ring in hole in the wall next to the bed. That way, he figured, if anyone came into the bedroom during the night to steal the ring he would wake up and catch the thief. The young couple slept soundly that night and when they woke up the next day they noticed the old man had repaired the flat tire and their car was waiting for them in front of the farmhouse. Before they drove off, they begged the old man to accept some payment for letting them spend the night and for fixing the flat tire, but he refused to accept their money. When they got to the Inn, and checked into the hotel they told the receptionist the story about what had happened to them that night and the man at the desk looked like he had seen a ghost.

"You must be mistaken" he said. "That house, the one you are describing, Metzger's farm, has been abandoned since I was a child. Nobody has lived there, or even been inside, since the gruesome murders took place there more than sixty years ago."

"Oh my God" exclaimed the young man. "The ring! I left it there. In the hole in the wall! We have to go back!"

Leaving the receptionist standing there holding out their room key, they jumped into their car and drove back to the farmhouse to try to find the ring. But when they got there, the farmhouse was exactly as you saw it today. Abandoned, boarded up and full of creepy, spiders. But the young man had to know if the engagement ring was in the hole in the wall next to the bed where he remembered putting it the previous night. So they took a rusty iron bar they found in the yard and pried off the 'No Trespassing' sign that had been nailed across the front door and broke into the farmhouse. With only a single match to light the way, they climbed the rotted staircase to the second floor where they saw the door to the bedroom where they had spent the night. Only this time it was covered with cobwebs and large chips of peeling crimson paint. After they forced the door open, they spilled into the room and saw the bed where they had slept. Throwing open a window so they could see, the couple searched frantically for the hole in the wall next to the bed, but it wasn't there. Maybe he had imagined the entire thing? But was it possible for both of them to have the same recollection? Just before they gave up looking, the man noticed a small picture hanging on the wall next to the bed. It was a picture of an old church. As he looked more closely at the picture he saw what looked like a shimmering light coming from somewhere inside the church. Carefully he took the picture off the wall to look at it more closely but as soon as he did the light went out. As he went to hang the picture back on the wall, he noticed a small hole behind where the picture had been, similar to the hole where he had remembered hiding the engagement ring. Carefully he put his finger in the hole and pulled out what looked like a long strand of cotton. When the cotton was no longer in the hole, he saw something twinkling in the dark recess of the cavity. He hoped it wasn't a spider. Reaching back into the hole he felt and pulled out his diamond engagement ring. As soon as they got back to the Inn, the man got down on one knee and asked his girlfriend to marry him and she said 'yes'. But nobody could explain what happened at Metzger's Farm on that dark and stormy night."

As soon as I finished the ghost story Veronica thought she heard something rustling in the woods down by the farmhouse. I didn't hear it but a few of the campers agreed with her. After she "shushed" everyone we listened to the silence of the woods and heard an owl hoot.

"Just a hoot owl" I told her. "Nothing to worry about."

"Not that" she said. "I heard something else. Like a thump, or a door closing."

"Now you're imagining things. There is nobody around for miles. C'mon kids. Grab your flashlights. Use the bathroom if you need to. Let's try to get a good night's sleep."

When I finished talking, nobody moved and we all heard what sounded like a branch breaking followed by a rock being moved in between us and the farmhouse.

"There's definitely something down there!" said Veronica starting to sound concerned. *"Why don't you go see what it is? Try to scare it away. I'll stay here with the campers."*

"Sure" I said, not wanting to show my concern. But in the back of my mind I was trying to remember what I was supposed to do if I came face to face with large wild animal, like a bear. There was a shovel by the latrine and a large kitchen knife in the cook kit but neither one seemed to offer much of a defense against 600 pound black bear which was not uncommon. Instead, I grabbed a large wooden spoon and a metal frying pan from the camp kitchen and walked down the hill into the darkness where I planned to make as much noise as possible before experiencing a terrible death. The beam of my flashlight, similar to what I'd seen in horror films, was ridiculously narrow and only illuminated what it was pointed directly at. So as I moved cautiously down the hill toward the area where the sounds were coming from, it was mostly pointed at the ground, so I wouldn't twist my ankle. The closer I got to the farmhouse, the louder the sounds got. Finally I was able to make out a shape in the darkness. It could have been a bear, but when I got within twenty feet of it I noticed it was standing on two legs,

like a person. As the beam from my flashlight swept across its face, I noticed it had a beard like the old man I had described in the ghost story. Or perhaps Sasquatch? Neither of which was good. Of course, that was when I dropped the flashlight and I heard a voice say,

"Who's there?"

"Me" I replied, which made absolutely no sense.

"Me, who?" the thing replied.

"Me, Daniel"

"Danny! the thing replied. *"It's me, Julian."*

"What the hell Julian!" I said. *"I thought you were a bear, or worse. Why didn't you drive up the road? It would have been a lot easier. And safer."*

"The gate was locked. I assume you locked it. Which is the right thing to do. You don't want just anybody driving up here at night interrupting your overnight. I brought Tommy Cullen's medicine. His mother told me he forgot to pack it. He needs to have one pill just before he goes to bed. She didn't tell me what it was for, but it I assume it's important. Otherwise I wouldn't have come all the way up here. Sorry to bother you. How are things with Veronica?"

"Same" I told him. *"She seems angry at me for some reason. Like it's my fault."*

"It's not your fault." he reassured me. *"She just doesn't know what she wants. It's not uncommon. Unfortunately, you will just have to wait around until she figures it out. Your balls are in her court."* After leaving me with these pearls of wisdom, Julian handed me a plastic bag that contained a single yellow pill and disappeared into the darkness.

Back at the campfire, I explained everything to Veronica and the campers, except the part about Tommy Cullen's medicine, and made sure everyone was where they were supposed to be and safely zipped inside their tents. Before I went to bed I tossed a couple of large logs onto the campfire hoping the flames would keep the animals away. As an added measure of security, I slept next to the frying pan and the large wooden spoon knowing they could be used to make noise and hopefully scare away any uninvited guests or as weapons of last resort.

The following afternoon, Bob Robertson had agreed to have lunch with my father's ex-wife in the main dining room of the Inn which, for Buck Hill Falls, was considered quite fancy. The best tables were on the far side of the restaurant next to the tall windows that overlooked the putting green and the pine forests that separated the Inn from Cottage 16 where I lived. As usual, Darlene Fitzpatrick had insisted on sitting at what was considered the premier table in the dining room so she could see people as they entered the room and be seen by everyone. For the most part, it had been a pleasant lunch until Darlene dabbed her lipstick with her cloth napkin and decided to get down to business.

"So Bob" she said. *"Now that we've caught up on pleasantries, there are a few things you need to explain. Rather than beat around the bush, I'm going come right out and ask. When am I going to get my money from my late husband's estate. And how much?"*

"Now Darlene, as I've already told you, these things take time. I understand you're upset, and if I were you, I might be feeling a little impatient right now."

"Impatient?! Bob, it's been seventeen years since Charles died or disappeared or ran away or whatever he did. I would hardly call that being impatient!"

"Darlene, please calm down. We're in a public place. You're absolutely right. You've not been impatient. You've been, well, let me see, what's the opposite of impatient?"

After a brief pause, Darlene threw up her arms and shouted *"PATIENT!"* causing the entire dining room to fall into a hushed silence. Lowering his voice, Bob answers her question.

"Well the good news is you should finally have your share of your late husband's estate in a few weeks, mid-September at the very latest."

"My share?" exclaimed Darlene *"What do you mean by 'share'?"*

Well, according to Webster's, a 'share' is a part or portion of a larger amount which is divided among a number of people."

"People? What people? His estate belongs to me! Throw me a bone here Bob and give me one good reason why I'm not getting every last dollar of my husband's estate?"

"Sure Darlene. I'd be glad to explain. To begin with, he wasn't exactly your husband when he went missing. You were legally separated, and there's a difference. As I'm sure you remember, his financial obligations were specified in the separation agreement. Secondly, he had a child. And because you and your team of

lawyers refused to agree to the generous terms of the divorce, years went by and the unfortunate boy was born out of wedlock. Since he was unable to be a proper father to the boy, it was his intention to leave a share of his estate to him, assuming the boy is able to live up to the moral's clause built into the trust agreement."

"Let's not forget that he made that money while we were still married. It's not my fault he couldn't keep his pecker in his pocket and got some sorry-ass cocktail waitress pregnant!"

Taken aback by her harshness, Bob signed the check but was unable to restrain himself.

"You have absolutely no right to criticize my best friend or the woman he happened to have fallen in love with. It wasn't like it was a one night stand. They'd been seeing each other for over a year and were planning to get married. I know, because he asked me to be his best man. That's right, Darlene! For the second time! How many times have you been married? I remember your first wedding, because I was there, but I didn't seem to get an invitation to any of the others. They must have gotten lost in the mail?

"Bob, please. Lower your voice. People are starting to stare."

"Let them stare. They started staring when you demanded to know how much money you were getting. Which is crass and frankly disgusting. Now they can stare when I stand up for my best friend, who can't stand up for himself. Because he's dead!"

I was completely exhausted when I got home from the overnight on Sunday afternoon. The night was uneventful, after Julian showed up. Tommy got his medicine and I slept with one eye open listening for any unusual sounds coming from the dark woods on the other sides of the thin membranes of our zippered nylon tents. After I ascended the winding staircase that Julian and I had started calling the "Hillary Step", after the nearly vertical rock face on top of Mount Everest, I dropped my backpack on the living room floor and passed out on the couch.

When I woke up nearly four hours later it was starting to get dark and I was beginning to get hungry. As usual, Julian wasn't nowhere to be found, so I scavenged around the kitchen and found a can of *Chef Boyardee Beefaroni* and heated it up on the stove in one of our two pots. After dinner I went back to my room which was a complete mess. My clothes were scattered all over the floor and there was a half empty bottle of Jack Daniels, without a cap, on the dresser where Veronica had left it before she suddenly dumped me. The smell of the whiskey brought back memories of our last night together. I remembered her sitting in the large armchair in the living room and the way she pulled her legs up in front of her trying to get comfortable. I loved it when she sneezed like a little cat and the way she would hide her face in her jacket whenever she did something cringe worthy. When I picked up my tee shirt that she had worn that night I could still smell the sweet, earthy scent of her perfume, *Obsession* by Calvin Klein.

The next week at Camp Club was pretty much business as usual. Veronica decided we should divide up the campers according to activities, so I took the kids who were interested in playing tennis to the tennis facility while she spent time at the pool supervising the swimmers. I tried not to take it personally, but this meant we would be spending a lot less time together. There really wasn't much for me to do while the kids were having tennis lessons, so I brought a book and got to know some of the kid's parents. One thing I realized, as I sat there on the tennis veranda overlooking the gray clay courts, was adults were just as cliquish as children, perhaps even more so. Certain people liked, or for some reason disliked, certain other people. Even if they went to the same schools or were members of the same club. You could tell by the way they interacted. For some reason, I liked almost everybody. I wasn't sure why, but people in general had always fascinated me. And when they did things I didn't expect, it often made them more fascinating. Up to a point. Some people, I learned much later in life, were just too complicated to try figure out.

At the end of the week it became clear why Veronica had decided we should divide and conquer. Her boyfriend Michael; he finally had a name, wanted to see where she worked and for her to show him around and she explained that it would be better for everyone, especially her, if our paths didn't cross. However, as fate would have it, our paths did cross. As we were saying goodbye to our campers on Friday afternoon, I noticed a brand new dark blue Toyota Supra with blacked out windows pulling up in front of the log cabin.

"*Oh my God!*" said Veronica holding her hand in front of her mouth. "*He came early. I can't believe it. Before you jump to conclusions, let me explain. Michael is in medical school. He happens to be brilliant. We went to high school together where he became obsessed with me. To be completely honest, I didn't mind the attention. He calls me his 'little panda'. We went to the junior and senior prom together and he's convinced we're going to be married someday. That's everything. Except the karate part. On weekends he teaches karate to underprivileged kids in the inner city and has a black belt."*

Michael was indeed my worst nightmare. How was I ever going to compete with that? Medical school was not in the cards for me. I was having enough trouble trying to figure out how to pay for college. I wanted to disappear, but it was too late and there was nowhere to hide. Time slowed to a crawl as the driver side door to the Toyota opened and we saw a small black and white snake skin loafer reach outside the door and step onto the pavement. Above the loafer was a bright yellow sock and an extremely tight pair of black skinny jeans worn by a diminutive Asian individual. As soon as he recognized Veronica his face lit up.

"Panda!" he shouted. *"My party girl. Like the new wheels?"*

After he gave her an awkward kiss on the lips, he turned toward me and said, *"Michael Yang, nice to meet you."* Before I was able to introduce myself, he looked back at her and told her she looked stressed and the good doctor was going to give her the best deep tissue shiatsu massage she'd ever had in her life as soon as they got to his room at the Inn. The power she had over him must have been intoxicating, because he didn't hear a single word she said to me when she apologized for not being able to go to the play that night.

As I walked back to Cottage 16 that afternoon I tried not to think about her getting a deep tissue massage from him, but I was unable erase the image of the two of them together in his hotel room. When I arrived at the cottage, I noticed someone had taped an envelope to the door with my name on it. It looked like Veronica's writing and inside was her ticket to the play that night and a short note saying she hoped I would be able to find someone to take her place. At first I wasn't sure if she was referring to filling her empty seat or finding another girlfriend. Then I realized it was probably both. When I gave her the ticket eight days ago, I had drawn a "smiley face" on the front side of the ticket and when I turned it over that afternoon, I saw she had drawn a "frowny face" on the back. Julian wasn't around, and I couldn't think of anyone to offer the ticket to, so I left it in the trash can that was sitting next to the garage.

Going to a play at the Pocono Playhouse was considered a big night out for most people in the Poconos and they tended to get dressed up. Other than the old tuxedo that I'd worn for the Wizard of Oz, the only dress clothes I had was the navy blue blazer that my mother bought me for graduation and a pair of tan pants. I didn't have a tie, but I also didn't have a date so I really didn't care. The original plan was for Veronica to drive us to dinner at her favorite Italian restaurant and then the Pocono playhouse. But now that Bruce Lee was in town, I had to figure out a way to get there. It was too far to walk and all the taxis had already been reserved.

Then I remembered someone had left a bicycle behind camp club a few weeks ago and must have forgotten it was there. The last time I checked the tires were good, so I walked down to Camp Club and borrowed the bike for the night. It was fine. Not perfect, but okay. I thought about removing the pink streamers from the handle grips, but at that point I really didn't care.

The Pocono playhouse was in Mountainhome and had been founded by a group of USO performers returning from World War II. Money must have been scarce because corners had obviously been cut and whatever building codes that existed at the time had obviously been circumvented. The box office and reception area looked like a hitching post from an old western attached to a shoe box with 497 seats positioned in front of a stage that looked like a repurposed high school gymnasium. Somehow, it all worked. Oftentimes the performers, who were on their way to Broadway, stayed in recreational vehicles parked out back. It was a good opportunity for them to polish their performances in front of a live audience before facing the critics who were sharpening their pencils for opening night in New York in just a few months.

After peddling for about 2 miles, I reached the dirt road that led up to the playhouse. Cars were already lining up and dropping passengers in front of the box office where a lighted sandwich board announced, "*Mousetrap! A murder mystery by Agatha Christie and the longest running play in London's West End.*" David McCallum, who had been in the hit television series *The Man from U.N.C.L.E.* was the lead actor that night and was playing a detective who arrives at an English manor the middle of snowstorm. The manor had been recently converted into a guesthouse and he questions the proprietors and the guests about a recent murder of a woman who lived nearby. The play has a "twist" ending and the sandwich board reminded anyone in the audience who might have seen the play before not to spoil the surprise at the end.

After I parked the pink Huffy BMX bicycle with the long banana seat next to a row of Harley Davidson motorcycles, I made my way inside the reception area where I saw a small bar with a long line. Even if I wanted to buy a drink I probably wouldn't have been able to get one because it looked like they were checking ID's. Although Bob Robertson would have happily ordered one for me. He was standing next to the bar talking to a coterie of friends with a cocktail in each hand and I wondered if he was holding one for someone else, or they were both for him. On the wall behind Bob and his entourage were autographed publicity pictures of actors who had performed at the playhouse including *Julie Andrews, Walter Matthau* and *Cybill Shepherd*.

I recognized quite a few faces in the crowd that evening. The general manager from the inn that Q had pointed out when I first arrived was entertaining a group of people who looked like they were from out of town. Karen Kelly's parents were there and it was impossible to look at Mr. Kelly without thinking about the singing frog who looked just like him and was wearing a tuxedo and a top hat in the commercials for Jack Kelly Motors. Mrs Bell was standing off to the side in the corner of the reception area with a woman from her tennis group holding a glass of white wine with two hands. She saw me, but as soon as our eyes met she quickly looked away. Even Mrs. Burdler was there taking pictures of the local celebrities who were attending the play that evening to post in the social column of the *Pocono Record* the following day.

As I was making my way across the crowded lobby toward Bob Robertson to say hello, the lights blinked twice indicating it was time for us to take our seats. After an usher helped me find my seat, an elderly woman, who looked a lot like Betty White, sat down beside me in what was supposed to be Veronica's seat. The evening was completely sold out and I guessed when they closed the doors to the theater they made an effort to use every available seat. I really didn't mind, but for some reason the woman who sat next to me took an aggressive position with the armrest and I had to scrunch over to one side of my chair to avoid the uncomfortable feeling of her body next to mine. Before the curtain went up I noticed her fanning herself and unbuttoning her blouse as if she was having some kind of a hot flash. I tried not to look over to see what was going on, but when I did I noticed she was wearing a revealing purple and black brassiere. Thankfully, after I saw more of her breasts than I wanted to remember, the lights went down and the curtain went up.

After the play was over and the performers received two standing ovations, I said hello to Bob Robertson who seemed in good spirits and introduced me to his friends who reminded me that we met at the cocktail party he had in his backyard earlier that summer. While we were talking, Mrs. Bell came over and introduced me to her friend who seemed to know Bob Robertson, and apparently my father, quite well.

I waited for the crowd to thin out before I retrieved my bicycle from behind the theater where I had left it earlier and got to meet some of the actors, including David McCallum who was sitting in a folding beach chair next to a large RV enjoying a cigarette. When he asked me if I enjoyed the show, I told him it was the best performance I'd ever seen, not mentioning to him that it was the only performance I had ever seen.

"*Well*" he said. "*Mistakes were made. We covered them up, that's what good actors do. But I'm glad you didn't notice. I know Agatha would not have been pleased. But I didn't see her in the audience.*" Everyone laughed but me, because I wasn't in on the joke. Agatha Christie had been dead for seven years. She died peacefully at her home in England at the age of 85.

It was a beautiful night and the only sounds were the rhythmic chirping of crickets and the back and forth croaking of frogs which sounded like nature's version of Marco Polo. I guess I had been spending too much time at the pool with eight year olds. As I flipped up the kickstand to my Huffy, I glanced up at the sky and saw a blanket of stars twinkling above me and, for the very first time in my life, I saw the hazy white band that was the Milky Way.

There weren't many cars on the road that night, but I decided to ride into oncoming traffic just in case someone wasn't paying attention and I needed to swerve out of the way. I was wearing dark clothing and I'd forgotten to bring a flashlight, so if I got hit by a car on the way home a case could be made that was at least partially my own fault.

As I rode past Maccioni's, where I knew Veronica and her boyfriend were having dinner, I noticed a couple having an argument in front of the restaurant. One of them was waving his arms back and forth trying to make a point while the other was listening patiently. My mother had warned me not to get involved with other people's problems, to let them work them out for themselves, but when he kicked over the trash can that was in the parking area, I decided to peddle to the other side of the street to take a closer look.

I was horrified when I recognized Veronica and her boyfriend. She was wearing a low cut black dress, that I hadn't seen before and he was wearing a dark blazer and a red sweater vest. They didn't see me at first, but I managed to capture their full attention when I swerved across the road and nearly got hit by a pickup truck. As Veronica did her best to wave me away, I noticed a crazed look come over her boyfriend's face.

"Incredible!" he said. *"Did you plan this? Talk about timing. Here comes your knight in shining armor on his trusted steed."*

"Michael, please!" Veronica begged, waving for me to stay away. *"He has nothing to do with any of this. We're just friends. That's all."*

It broke my heart to hear her say this and I wanted to shout at the top of my lungs that Veronica and I had been lovers, and not just once, but time and time again. Instead, I just stood there looking at her, waiting for her eyes to tell me what I should do. When the signal from her never came, he waved me off with his hand, as if I was some stray dog that had wandered onto his property looking for food.

"Go ahead" he said. *"Go on home. We're having a private conversation here. You heard what she said. It has nothing to do with you. So we're asking you nicely, please leave."*

When I found myself unable to move, he took a step toward me and I flipped down the kickstand of my bike signaling I wasn't going to leave until I was sure that Veronica was safe. Then I remembered he was a black belt in karate. Was her boyfriend actually going to punch me, I remember thinking. I'd never been in a real fight before, so I wasn't sure if I should raise my hands to protect my face or my body? Whatever he did next, I guessed, would determine my next move. Before I knew what was happening he was standing directly in front of me so close that I could smell the garlic on his breath from whatever he had eaten for dinner.

"Have it your way. If you're not going to leave, I guess that means we're going to settle this with our hands. You should punch me first, because after I break both your arms, I can say you threw the first punch. Pick you spot. Face is good. Or stomach. Doesn't matter to me."

Even though Michael was more than a foot shorter than me, there was no way I was going to start a fight with him. Finally, Veronica stepped in and tried to push us apart.

"This is not happening" she said. *"Michael. Take me home. Right now!"*

When I leaned over to pick up the trash can he had knocked over, he shouted, *"Leave it!"* Ignoring what he said, I reached down and the last thing I saw, before I blacked out, was his snake-skin loafer coming up toward my face.

The next thing I remembered, was someone was shining a flashlight in my eyes asking me what my name was. After I answered them correctly, they wanted to know what day it was and I told them it was Friday. *"And the year?"* they asked. *"1981"* I told the light.

"Well, he doesn't seem to have a concussion" said a woman in a blue uniform with a stethoscope around her neck. When she helped me sit up, I noticed I had been taken inside the restaurant and was surrounded by a group of people with concerned looks on their faces. Even Veronica's boyfriend looked concerned.

"I want you to know. I'm really sorry." he said. *"I wasn't trying to kick you. I was aiming for the garbage can. And I missed. It was an accident. And I apologize."* I wasn't sure if he really meant it, or was trying to convince the crowd, which now included two police officers, that it had been an accident. All I knew was my head was pounding and the clothes I had worn to the play were now covered with what I assumed was my own blood. When I saw my reflection in the restaurant window, I noticed someone had stuffed bandages inside my nose which had swollen to twice it's normal size.

After the paramedics left, the police took us over to a table in the back of the restaurant and questioned us about what had happened. An older couple had witnessed the entire scene, and they had already written down their testimony, so the officers told us all we needed to do was confirm what they already knew and perhaps explain to them, "why?". When we were done, they asked me if I wanted to press charges and I told them 'no'.

We were all asked to take breathalyzer tests and since Michael was double the legal limit for alcohol they took away his car keys. The fact that he was drunk *and* had been involved in assault and battery meant he would have to spend the night in jail at the police station.

"*It's not as bad as it sounds.*" the female officer reassured Michael. "*Not like Midnight Express. You'll be the only one there. We've all slept there on occasion when we want to get away from our spouses. There's a comfortable cot with clean sheets. Your own toilet, in case you feel sick. We just want to make sure everyone cools down and has a safe night.*"

After Michael apologized to Veronica and looked like he was about to cry, he gave me what appeared to be a concerned pat on the shoulder and told me he was glad that I was fine. Which, we all knew, I wasn't. After that, one of the officers helped him into the back of the cruiser and hauled him away to his "comfortable cot" at the Mountainhome police station.

At that point, the only people left at the restaurant were the owner, who was anxious to lock up and go home, Veronica, an older police officer with a moustache that made him look like a walrus, and me. When the walrus asked me if I needed a ride home I told him I was fine.

"It's not far, and I could use some air to clear my head." Just to be sure, he asked me a second time and after I reassured him I was fine, he loaned me his flashlight in hopes that he wouldn't get a second call that night that someone needed to be peeled off the pavement.

Turning his attention to Veronica, he asked, *"What about you missy? You've had a rough night. You gonna walk home with your boyfriend or do you want me to give you a lift?"*

Nothing could have made me happier than him mistaking me for Veronica's boyfriend, and she didn't seem to have the energy or feel the need to correct him.

"I'm fine. I'll walk home with Danny" she told him. *"I need to make sure he gets home okay. It's the least I can do, after what happened. We'll be fine, but thanks for the offer."*

After the police car drove off and Mr. Maccioni turned off the lights to the restaurant, I went back to the parking lot and retrieved the Huffy bike that was standing innocently in the middle of the parking lot as if nothing had happened. After I flipped the kickstand back into its upright position, Veronica and I walked in silence for what seemed like an eternity. I honestly don't think either of us would have said a word to each other that night if she hadn't stepped in a pothole and twisted her ankle.

"Ouch!" she cried.

"Are you okay?" I asked as I helped her get back on her feet. *"I'm fine"* she said. *"Just tired. It's been a really long night."* When I offered her the Huffy bike, she shook her head and said, *"The way things are going tonight, I'd probably fall off."*

After about 100 yards walking became too painful, so Veronica took the flashlight from me and climbed onto the back of my pink Huffy BMX bike and wrapped her arms around my waist and allowed me to peddle us both home.

I spent the next day holding bags of ice on my cheekbones and packing my nose with cotton balls so I wouldn't bleed on my clothes and the furniture. Julian thought I should see a doctor, but I told him I'd already seen one and things hadn't worked out so well. I hoped that Veronica would stop by to make sure I was okay, but when she didn't and I imagined she had problems of her own dealing with her boyfriend who had spent the night in jail hoping I hadn't derailed his medical career by allowing my nose to be broken by his loafer.

By the time Monday rolled around, the bruises on my face were beginning to turn a purplish, yellow color. At the staff meeting, when the other counselors asked what had happened to me, I told them I'd gotten into an argument with a trash can. Molly, the senior girls counselor commented, *"It looks like you lost"* and I told her she was not incorrect. Everyone knew there was more to the story than what I was letting on, but they also could tell that I wasn't ready to talk about it.

Toward the middle of the week, Julian rounded up the staff and had us sit on the picnic tables behind Camp Club while he lectured us about what a good job we had been doing which, from the way it sounded to me, was his way of patting himself on the back for managing us. Years later, I realized he must have been pretty lonely that summer because there was nobody who was his age that he could hang around with and as long as nothing bad happened, nobody ever came by to ask him how things were going or tell him that he was doing a good job.

"With only two weeks left in the summer, we have not had one single hospitalization or major incident. No whooping cough, lice, ticks, parasites, Malaria, Dengue fever, Tuberculosis, Scarlet Fever, Typhoid, River blindness, Guinea worm syndrome, Waterhouse-Friderichsen. All negative. Other than Willie Wilson getting a fishhook stuck in his finger, that I had to remove by snipping off the barb and pulling it through the side of his thumb, we have a perfect record. With only a few weeks left I want to remind everyone to keep up the good work. It is my hope that we end this summer with a bunch of happy campers. In other words, don't screw up."

As I walked back up the hill to Cottage 16 to wash up, Karen and Q drove by in a car I hadn't seen before. It was a brand new Chevy Camaro Z28 with a removable a T-top that was made famous by the movie *Smokey and the Bandit*. When they saw me she stopped and leaned out the window and asked me if I wanted to go with them to Harrisburg where she had to pick up some parts for her father. I didn't have anything better to do, so I hopped in the back seat.

As Karen pushed the car well beyond the posted speed limit, Q told me things at the Inn were coming to a head. "*Szabo is pushing us to default on the bank loan. That way, his friends in Atlantic City will be able to buy it for pennies on the dollar from their relatives at Susquehanna S&L so they can turn it into a "family business". Mind you, I got nothing against casinos. Been to a few myself and handed over more cabbage than I care to talk about. It's not what they're doing, it's how they're doing it. If they somehow pull this off, I get shoved aside but my name and my fingerprints and my reputation stay in the phony ledger books forever. Let me ask you something, would you be able to sleep at night waiting for a time bomb like that to go off? I've seen some of the plans. They want to turn this place into a convention center and as soon as the stripper poles arrive, Camp Club becomes Strip Club. This place will never be the same.*"

I knew Q was a nervous guy, but now he was starting to sound paranoid. As I sat in the back seat of the Camaro going 90 miles an hour down a deserted stretch of highway, I couldn't help but wonder why he was telling me all this? Or if it was even true. I liked Q, and we had spent some time together, but I really didn't know him. What if this was all something that was going on in his head. What if he was on some kind of medicine that stopped working? Some of the things he was saying sounded absurd. Plus there wasn't anything I could do to stop the chain of events, if there even was a "chain of events". After he stopped talking, I asked him if he wanted me to mention something to Bob Robertson which only made him more anxious.

"Promise me you won't say a word to anyone! My gut tells me a few of the Cottagers are in on the deal and may have been paid off. I'm not sure who we can trust."

Just when I thought things couldn't get any weirder, shortly after they dropped me off at Cottage 16, Julian came up the stairs and asked me if I wanted to get high. He'd just gotten some weed from Humboldt County in Northern California and wanted to try it out. When I told him I'd never gotten high before, he told me it was something I needed to experience before going off to college. Since it was just going to be the two of us, he reassured me if I experienced anything strange, he would be there next to me to help me get through it.

Julian had great taste in music and after he put on an album named *Moonbathing* by an obscure English folk singer named Leslie Duncan, we went out to the balcony where there was a small wooden table and two deck chairs. The third floor balcony was high enough so nobody could see us through the branches of the pine trees and the light breeze that was blowing that night would help carry away the smoke. Like everything he did, Julian was meticulous about the way he separated the seeds and the stems from his newly acquired stash on the gatefold of a double album by the Rolling Stones. When he was happy with what remained, he picked up a ball of the weedy mixture and pushed it into the bowl of the bong making sure it wasn't packed too tightly. After he placed his mouth inside the opening on top of the water pipe, he lit the mixture with his BIC lighter and pulled the smoke into the glass chamber. Once the chamber was full the bubbling stopped and he released his finger from a small hole on the side of the pipe and breathed the smoke deeply into his lungs. I wouldn't go so far as to say the Humboldt County weed smelled good, but it smelled a whole lot better than the dead skunk aroma we experienced that day when my mother and my grandfather had dropped me off.

After Julian exhaled, he cleaned out the bowl with a small wire brush and refilled it with another plug of the pungent green mixture that was sitting on the table next to me.

"*Your turn*" he said as he presented me with the bong as if it was a trophy of some kind. Even though I had just watched him smoke the pipe expertly, I had a hard time figuring out what to do. After he told me where to put my mouth and pointed to where the air hole was, he held a flame over mixture and I pulled the smoke into the glass chamber. Despite his coaching, my timing was off and most of the smoke that I pulled into the glass tube escaped out the sides of the pipe when I attempted to breathe it into my lungs. Whatever smoke I was able to inhale was quickly exhaled when I had a sudden coughing fit.

While I recovered, Julian took the bong from me and repeated the steps he had taken earlier and took another, perfectly timed, hit from the pipe. When he offered me the pipe for the second time, I shook my head and told him I was okay for now. He was fine with that. We were sharing a moment, and even though I hadn't successfully mastered the bong, I felt a warm relaxed feeling come over me as we sat there like birds in a nest on the third floor balcony.

I wasn't sure if I was high or not, but it was obvious Julian was. He seemed both far away and close at the same time and nobody said a word as we sat there listening to his music and the whispering breezes that blew gently through the branches of the tall pine trees. Finally he asked what had happened the night of the play, and after I told him the whole story, he said he was really sorry about the way things had turned out

"Veronica's not a bad person." he said. *"I'm glad you two connected. She's just young and it's clear she doesn't know what she wants. Change can be a real bitch. One of the greatest causes of human suffering is our inability to accept change. I'm not saying it's over between the two of you. It might be. Or it might not be. People get stuck wanting things to be a certain way. But more often than not, life has other plans for you. Whenever I get stuck, I think about that nursery rhyme we sang in school. The one that goes...'Row, row, row your boat, gently down the stream, merrily, merrily, merrily, life is but a dream.' The key to life is, never stop rowing."*

Maybe I actually was high, because all I could think about was food. The hamburgers at the Inn were pretty good and they came with French fries, potato chips and a large dill pickle. I hadn't been eating much since Veronica and I split up but now I was suddenly starving. From what I had observed, Julian appeared to be a vegetarian, but I wasn't really sure so I invited him to join me at the Pub in the Inn for a hamburger. He didn't seem offended, and he thanked me for the offer but said he had plans for the evening.

Most of the tables at the King's Arms were occupied that night, so I found a seat at the end of the bar and ordered the hamburger that I had been craving and a draft beer hoping I wouldn't get carded. The bartender remembered me from Bob Robertson's cocktail party and, I'm pretty sure, the Kelly's Fourth of July barbeque; the details of which were still a little foggy in my brain, so getting a beer that night wasn't a problem. The bacon cheeseburger was seared on the outside and pink in the middle, just the way I liked it, and the lettuce was crisp inside a soft warm bun. The fries were great too, and the pickle snapped when I sunk my teeth into it.

I don't think it was the weed, but it could have been, because the cheeseburger that night was the best I ever tasted. The more I thought about what Julian had said about letting go, the more I began to realize that I would probably never hold Veronica in my arms again.

Hanging on the wall behind the bar was a pair of dueling pistols. When I asked the bartender about them he told me they were identical to the ones that belonged to Alexander Hamilton, the former Secretary of the Treasury, who was killed by his longtime political rival and adversary Aaron Burr who was the sitting Vice President of the United States.

"That's the way people used to settle arguments in those days. Duels followed a strict code of conduct and were a generally accepted practice up until around 1859. More often than not, people didn't die in a duel. It was customary for both participants to fire their first shot into the ground, at which point a man's honor would be restored. However, instead of firing into the ground, Hamilton fired above Burr's head hitting a tree branch behind him. Burr saw this as an indication that there could be no reconciliation between the two men, so he took aim and shot Hamilton in the abdomen causing him to die the following day. These days we hire lawyers to settle our differences, which causes more pain and suffering than a lead ball the size of an olive."

After I got home that night and went to sleep I had a lucid dream that Michael and I had agreed to a duel on the putting green behind the Inn at dawn. In my dream Michael was tall and handsome and looked like George Washington. We were both wearing powdered wigs and tricorn hats and the bartender from the King's Arms was explaining the codes of conduct but Michael wasn't paying attention to a word he was saying. Instead, Michael was blowing kisses to Veronica who was standing off to the side dressed like Marie Antoinette and holding hands with Julian, who was wearing a robe with a fur collar that looked a lot like Louis the XVI. Neither of them seemed the least bit interested in what was about to happen.

After the bartender examined our pistols and made sure they were cocked and loaded, he handed one to each of us and explained the rules of engagement.

"As you can see, the pistols are identical" he explained. *"Each weapon is capable of firing two shots. After I count off ten paces you both will turn, face each other and discharge your weapons. Once you have both fired your first shot, honor will be considered restored. However, if either of you is still not satisfied, you may choose to fire a second shot. The first to person to draw blood will be considered the winner. Prepare to start your paces on my count. One, two..."*

After he counted off ten paces, I turned around and instead of seeing an Asian George Washington staring down the barrel of a gun, I saw a fly fisherman who, from Bob Robertson's description looked like my father. He appeared to be about my age, maybe several years older, and as soon as saw me he smiled and waved. In between us, where the putting green had been, was a shallow river that made a rushing sound as it spilled over the mossy rocks. For a moment we just stood there looking at each other until he appeared to remember there was something he wanted to tell me. I saw his lips moving but the rushing sound of the river made it impossible for me to hear what he was saying.

Saturday, Sunday and Monday were uneventful and other than it raining the entire day on Tuesday, forcing us to dig out the board games from the arts and crafts closet, I honestly can't remember a single thing that happened on any of those days. Wednesday, however, it looked like my string of bad luck was finally coming to an end. That night, when I was working my way through Julian's eclectic music collection and having "breakfast for dinner" by myself, the phone rang and on the other end of the line was Phoebe. Just hearing her voice was like a ray of sunshine coming out from behind a wall of dark storm clouds. After she filled me in on what everyone had been up to since I left town two and a half months ago, she asked if I was sitting down and ready for some good news. Her sister had booked their band, now called *T Bone and the Girl*, at the *Wobbly Tavern* which was less than a half hour away in Stroudsburg. The show was Friday night and a German heavy metal rock band named *The Scorpions* was supposed to play, but they were having bus trouble in Birmingham, Alabama and had to cancel at the last minute. Phoebe said she and Tony had been practicing day and night for the last six weeks and it was time to take their show on the road and see how they performed in front of live audiences. When she asked how many tickets I wanted, I was embarrassed to tell her that I only needed one, so I said four, but as soon as I hung up I began to worry about what to do with the three extra tickets.

The next day, after the Camp Club staff meeting, Veronica gave me a funny look and asked me why I looked so happy. When I said "nothing in particular" it aroused her suspicions that I was hiding something, which I suppose I was. Since the first day of June, Veronica and I had been practically inseparable. I wouldn't be exaggerating if I said that we had spent almost every waking moment together and, until last week, more than a few of our sleeping moments. We had learned to read each other's body language and moods and it was almost as if we could tell what the other person was thinking. There were times when I had to bite my tongue not to finish her sentences for her. Which explains why I was so blown away that she had been able to keep her boyfriend a secret from me for so long. Somehow, she'd been able to keep him locked away where nobody could see him, which only made me wonder what other secrets might be sequestered in the dark recesses of her mind? I guess we all have secrets we would rather not share with anyone, even our closest friends and lovers. If I was reading her mind correctly that morning, I would say she was wondering how I managed to get over her so quickly and seemed to be moving ahead with my life. Julian was right, Veronica wasn't a bad person. She didn't want me to feel bad after she dumped me, she just didn't want me to feel good.

I tried to hide my excitement about reuniting with my friends by thinking sad thoughts whenever Veronica was around, but by the end of the day she couldn't stand the suspense and came right out and asked me what was going on.

"So, what's up? you look like the cat that swallowed the canary. Are you going to tell me what you're up to, or are you just going to torture me until someone else spills the beans?"

I must have still had feelings for her, because I knew her mind wouldn't stop racing until it came up with a plausible explanation for my sudden surge of happiness.

"My friends are coming this weekend. The ones I told you about, Phoebe and Tony. Their band is playing at the Wobbly Tavern tomorrow night and I'm going to be able to see them play. Will and Doug might come too. So we're all going to be together. I would have asked you to go, but wasn't sure how Michael would feel about me asking you."

"Phoebe? I forget, who's this Phoebe person?" she asked.

"My friend from home. The one who sings in a band."

"Oh yeah. Now I remember. The girl you have a crush on."

"A secret crush. She's dating my best friend. I told you that in confidence. During Truth or Dare. You swore not to tell anyone. Or I might have to tell people about your girl crush.

"Fine. We know each other's secrets. Anyway, why are we talking about Phoebe?"

"Because she's performing at the Wobbly Tavern tomorrow night with my best friend Tony. Her boyfriend. I'm thinking about asking Q and Karen if they want to go. You can come too if you want. There's going to be a group of us, so it's not like we'd be going on a date.

After thinking about my invitation for a moment she said, *"Sure. Why not? I'd love to meet your secret girlfriend and go to the Wobbly Tavern. I've never been there, and I've always wanted to go. So it's a date. Actually, it's not a date. It's a group thing. Not a date."*

"Exactly" I said. *"They go on at 9:00 and I have four tickets. If Q and Karen can go, he will probably want to drive. So I'll let you know how we are getting there."*

For the first time in over a week I thought I saw her smile.

I'd almost forgotten that I had promised Bob Robertson I would come over for another one of his famous steak dinners that night. People ate a lot of meat back then. Especially Bob. In fact, the only people that I knew who were vegetarians were hippies and radicals. And I guess grilling meat outdoors seemed to appeal to Bob's inner caveman.

We ate our steaks and baked potatoes at a small table in the backyard that night, and before he had too much to drink, I asked him if he could tell me some stories about my father. What he was like when he was around my age.

"Your father was a bit of a loner when we first met." Bob told me. *"Very devoted to his studies. He kept to himself. I had to practically drag him out of the library on weekends to go to parties at the supper club where I belonged. I was a legacy at Princeton and treasurer of the Cottage Club, one of the most exclusive supper clubs on campus. The list of famous members is a long as your arm and we counted F. Scott Fitzgerald as one of our own. Scottie described us as a bunch of 'brilliant adventurers and well-dressed philanderers'. In the dining room, just above the fireplace is a carved wooden panel that says 'Where there are friends, there are riches."*

"Twice a year, Princeton has these events called 'lawn parties' where the supper clubs open their doors to the campus for a full day of drinking and carrying on. I talked your dad into having a drink at each of the eleven clubs and it became an odyssey of Homeric proportions. Without going into the details, he was able to convince two perfect strangers not to fight over a girl they were

both attracted to, washed a piece of glass out of this poor chaps eye who surely would have lost his sight, met an enchantress named Ruby and passed out behind the couch in the library on the second floor of Cottage. Never much of a drinker, when he woke up the next day he couldn't remember a single thing that had happened.

"So it goes without saying that I miss your father dearly. If I had to use one word to describe him, it would be 'authentic'. What you saw was what you got. He accepted himself for what he was, and not for what he was not. We're all imperfect. We just don't want to admit it. Look at me. I can be a pompous ass. Still talking about Princeton and supper clubs. I can't speak for women, but every man I know still feels like he's in his early to mid-twenties. Nobody wants to admit they are getting older. We all want to hang onto our youth as long as possible. You can call it denial, but I call it a gift from God. Intelligent design. Allowing us to believe that we're still young right up until we take our last breath. Hopefully, at a very old age."

As I was preparing to leave, he remembered something he wanted to tell me.

"I'm having a birthday soiree for my niece Amber next week and I'd like you to come. She's turning 30, and like me, she doesn't have someone special in her life. It must run in the family. Most of my friends are older than Methuselah, so I thought I'd invite a few people closer to her age. She's a real peach. Smart cookie too. Graduated from Columbia. I got her a position in the U.S. Attorney's office working under Tony Bell. You know, Briny's father."

Before I left, he showed me a picture of his niece and it was hard to imagine a woman that intelligent and attractive didn't have someone special in her life. Then I remembered Briny telling me about a woman named Amber who worked with his father and was making his mother unhappy. Amber wasn't a common name. Was Bob's niece the reason Mr. Bell wasn't spending much time at Buck Hill? Or was I jumping to conclusions? Whatever was, or wasn't going on, I felt myself being pulled into the unfolding drama of the Bell's family.

After I got back from Camp Club on Friday afternoon, I heard the rotary phone ringing somewhere underneath the couch where it lived and when I answered, it was Tony Bagnoli.

"*Danny!*" he shouted into the phone. "*We made it. We're in Stroudsburg at a place called the Wobbly Willie, or something like that, and we just finished setting up. It's a dive bar, you're going to love it! I want to make sure Phoebe reached out and you're going to show up. We're practically in your backyard, brother.*"

After I told him Phoebe had called two days ago and I was bringing three friends, he said he was going to leave four comped covers at the front door with a bouncer named T-Rex.

I heard the low rumbling sound of Q's Firebird waiting in the driveway and when I came downstairs I saw that they had already picked up Veronica and she was wedged in the back seat behind Q wearing a black spandex miniskirt and an off the shoulder denim top. She looked great and after I squeezed in beside her she thanked me for inviting her to join us.

"*I was hoping I'd get to meet your friends.*" she told me as we listened to "*Take The Long Way Home*" by Supertramp playing on the 8 track tape player in the center console of Q's car. We drank beer in the backseat as Q drove south on route 191 and eventually hooked a left onto Sarah street where the Wobbly Tavern had been located since it became a music venue in 1961.

At the door was a heavily tattooed man who must have weighed at least 350 pounds.

Feeling confident, I walked up to the man and said "*You must be T-Rex?*"

"*Nope*" he said. "*First time at the Wobbly? Cause I look nothing like T-Rex. My name is Tiny. It's not a nickname. It's the name my mama gave me. Because I was a small baby.*"

If the largest man I had ever seen didn't look like T-Rex, then Mr. Rex must be a giant.

"*You're right*" I said. "*It's our first time. We're friends of the band. They said they left our tickets with Mr. Rex. So if you could...*"

Before I could finish he said "*Hang on*" and disappeared inside the club. A few moments later he came back with an envelope with my name on it. After he opened the envelope, he tore the tickets in half, handed me the stubs and stamped our wrists with an image of a dinosaur.

"*So that must be T-Rex.*" I said trying to make a joke.

"*Wrong again*" he said. "*That is a Brontosaurus. T-Rex is the owner of the establishment. He's not around much. But in case he shows up, I'll describe him, so you don't go around asking everyone you meet if they are T-Rex. He's a little guy. With very small arms. If you happen to see him, whatever you do, don't say anything about the length of his arms. Enjoy the show."*

The Tavern itself had been operating since before the American Revolution. A long bar ran along the entire left side of the room and to the right was a dining area with groupings of wooden tables positioned around a small dance floor in front of a small stage.

We had gotten there early so we didn't have any problem securing a good table in the middle of the room that wasn't too close to the speakers. As I looked around at all the empty tables, and the handful of regulars hunched over their drinks at the bar, I hoped more people would show up so my friends wouldn't have to perform in front of a half empty room.

After the hostess handed out menus and told us which local beers were on tap. I asked her if the band had arrived and she told me they were hanging out in the back room eating pizza.

"Blue door behind the stage" she said.

The back room was used for private functions and had a pool table and groupings of well-worn leather club chairs. I wasn't absolutely sure, but off to the side was what looked like a dance pole from a Gentleman's Club. There was a cover on the pool table where the instruments were laid out next to a blackboard with the playlist for the evening written in chalk.

It had only been a few months since we were all together but it seemed like a year. Tony had grown a beard and moustache that made him look like a 'beatnik'. Phoebe had colored the tips of her hair pink and looked even more beautiful than I had remembered. We were excited to see each other, and I could tell they were nervous about performing that night. Doug had enlisted in the Army and had been away at boot camp for six weeks. He had a flat top haircut, had lost weight and was wearing a military green tee shirt. Will's reddish brown hair was now shoulder length, and he was on his way to his first semester at Virginia Tech in a Ford Econoline van that he picked up at a junkyard for next to nothing and repaired.

After we caught up, we laughed about the name they had picked for the band: *"T-Bone and the Girl"*. Phoebe said she would have preferred equal billing, but Tony talked her out of it.

"That way, when I decide to start my solo career, Tony won't have to change the name of his band. He just needs to find another 'Girl'."

When Phoebe asked me about my friends, I suddenly remembered I had told them I would be right back and that was nearly a half an hour ago. Everyone urged me to bring them backstage, so I went back to the table and invited them to meet the band. After I introduced my friends to Q and Karen and Veronica, Phoebe asked Veronica if she wouldn't mind helping her with her makeup and the two of them disappeared into the private bathroom. Hair and makeup must be a lot more complicated than I realized, because the two of them were gone for at least a half an hour and Veronica got back to the table just as the band was about to take the stage.

The set began with a guitar riff by Tony covering *The Boys are Back in Town* by *Thin Lizzy,* which he figured was a crowd pleaser. The room was half empty when they started, but as soon as Phoebe took the microphone and began to sing I saw one of the regulars who had been sitting by himself at the bar get up and start feeding quarters into the payphone by the restroom calling a few of his friends. Less than fifteen minutes later, the room was packed.

Standing alone in the light of a single spotlight Phoebe covered a song by Bob Seger called *Blue Monday.* She crushed it. As soon as she finished singing, the band kicked into *In the Midnight Hour* by Wilson Pickett followed by a cover of *Crossfire* by Stevie Ray Vaughan where Tony wore a black Cowboy hat, similar to the one Stevie Ray had worn, and got to show off his improvisational guitar style.

After that, the band took a short break and returned to start the second set off with *Born under a bad sign* by Albert King. By the end of the night there wasn't an inch of space on the dance floor and Tiny had to wedge himself into the doorway in order to keep people out. Before the last song of the night, Phoebe asked the audience to quiet down and told everyone she had a special announcement.

"Tonight has been a really special evening for us. It's the first night of our eight city tour, and I know I speak for everyone when I say what a pleasure it has been to kick things off right here in Stroudsburg! It is your energy that powers us. Thank you! Tell your friends! Since you've been such a great audience, we have a special treat for you. Joining us for the last song of the evening is a brave and talented woman who will be making her first stage appearance since, I don't know, high school? We practiced this

song together only once earlier this evening, so if you will, please put your hands together for Lady V!"

I almost fell off my chair when Veronica got up and joined Phoebe on the stage. It was beyond brave. It was suicidal. I had no idea she could sing or was confident enough to perform in front of a live audience. On top of that she didn't seem nervous at all. She held a small scrap of paper in her hand, which I assumed were the lyrics, and when Tony played the first few notes I recognized the song they were about to sing. *Chain of Fools* by Aretha Franklin.

Chain, chain, chain
Chain, chain, chain
Chain, chain, chain
Chain of fools
For five long years
I thought you were my man
But I found out
I'm just a link in your chain
You got me where you want me
I ain't nothin' but your fool

You treated me mean

Oh, you treated me cruel.

Phoebe and Veronica's duet was too much for the audience to handle and as soon as they stopped singing the crowd started chanting, "*More, more, more.*"

Eventually, Tony had to come out of the back room to tell everyone "*There is no more to pour. Goodnight!*" After the bar emptied out, we ate cold pizza and drank coffee until just past three AM when Phoebe reminded Tony they had to drive to Baltimore, check into the Holiday Inn and try to get some rest before playing again that night. After we said goodbye and wished them luck, we climbed back into Q's car and drove home along the deserted winding roads.

When I woke up the next day, I made myself a strong cup of coffee and walked out to the balcony to sit in the warm sunlight that was filtering through the pine branches. As I sat there in the stillness of the afternoon, I sensed a familiar coolness in the air that reminded me that September was just around the corner and summer was slipping quietly out the backdoor. The perennial gardens that surrounded the Inn had started to lose their luster but the late bloomers, particularly the orange and red marigolds that lined the road up to the Inn were hanging in there and continued to glow in the late summer sun.

Veronica hadn't said a word about her boyfriend since he accidently shattered my nose in the parking lot almost two weeks ago. Complete radio silence. She didn't bring it up, and I didn't ask. For all I knew he was still in jail. But that probably wasn't the case, because the day after the trash can incident I noticed his car had disappeared from Maccioni's parking lot. Even though we had a great time at the Wobbly Tavern that night, whatever "heat" had once been simmering in our relationship was no longer there.

In the middle of the week, while we were watching the kids play kickball on the field behind camp club, Veronica looked over at me and said, "*We need to talk.*"

"*Okay*" I said, setting down the Rubik's cube that I had been trying unsuccessfully to figure out all summer, and prepared myself for the worst.

"I've been thinking a lot lately, and I should have told you about Michael. I'm not sure why I didn't tell you about him. Perhaps because I was being selfish. I wanted you both. I've known

Michael since we were in high school. When I had problems, he seemed to have all the answers. But he became controlling. And he stopped listening. And the conversations became mostly about him. And I felt myself slowly disappearing. I didn't want to just be somebody's crush, I wanted someone to like and know the real me. That's what we were arguing about. Somewhere, in the middle of dinner, we both knew it was over. We'd come to the end of the road and there was nothing either one of us could do about it. It was excruciating."

After I thanked her for what seemed like an apology, or an admission of guilt, I'm not sure which, she got up and left. Since I never had a relationship that lasted more than several weeks, I couldn't fully appreciate what she was talking about, but I did my best to understand. When she first dropped the bomb on me that she had a boyfriend, I was furious because the thing I most admired about her was her honesty. Then, my anger gave way to disappointment and a bruised feeling in my heart that I wasn't sure would ever go away. Ever since my mother had told me that my father had abandoned us when I was a child, I set my expectations lower than I probably should have fearing things would not work out. As a result, up until that point, my history of rejection had been limited to things like being picked last when choosing sides for kickball. There were plenty of girls I had wanted to date in high school, but I wouldn't ask them out because I was afraid they would say "no" or make up some lame excuse so I wouldn't feel bad, which would make me feel even worse. Instead, I went for the girls who wanted to go to the prom, but couldn't find a date. Even then, more often than not, their acceptance had been prearranged and virtually guaranteed by not one but as many as three of their closest friends.

Despite having anger management issues, which could probably be mitigated over time with therapy, Michael Yang had many gifts and advantages that I didn't have. He was intelligent enough to recognize how unique and special Veronica was and had enough self-confidence to actually believe that he could win her heart. Even if he failed, his determination was admirable. As a doctor, he would be an excellent provider. Michael would live in a beautiful home in a nice neighborhood with an attractive wife and their intelligent children who would be dropped off at the right schools in a sporty but sensible car and be taught karate by their attentive father.

By dating both of us at the same time, and not telling one about the other, Veronica was beginning to understand that sometimes when you try to have it all, you end up with nothing.

It had been a long week and I really wasn't in the mood to go to the birthday party that Bob was throwing for his beloved niece, so I planned to stop by and say hello, grab some food and leave early. BBN, older people called it. Bed by nine. It was getting dark when I arrived at Bob's cottage and I saw a row of Tiki torches flickering in his backyard below several strings of red Japanese lanterns. The meandering stone walkway that led to his backyard was illuminated by candles and when I arrived at his garden patio I noticed there were two bars attended by four bartenders from the Inn. That way, Bob's guests didn't have to ask for a drink because the men already knew what everyone drank and exactly how they liked their cocktails prepared.

When Bob noticed me standing at the bar picking up my ginger ale, he came over with an older couple he had been having a conversation with.

"Danny. I want to introduced you to my close friends, Babs and Bulkie Prescott. Bulkie's great grandfather invented the

cocktail wiener, and for that we are eternally grateful. If you are nice to him he might give you a key chain that looks like the Weiner mobile. I have several."

The Prescott's could not have been nicer, but when Mrs. Prescott asked me where I "Wintered" I had absolutely no idea what she was talking about. Thankfully, Bob's golfing buddy Albert Hall came over and took over the conversation.

Identifying Bob's niece wasn't too difficult. The only person even close to my age was an attractive brunette wearing a plastic tiara with fake diamonds that spelled out *"Birthday Girl"*.

Ever the gracious host, Bob grabbed me by the arm and hauled me over to introduce us.

"Danny, allow me to introduce you to my favorite niece Amber. Amber, this is the young man I've been telling you about. Daniel Barnes. His father was one of my closest friends. Danny is going to be a freshman at William & Mary and has been working at Camp Club this summer where I hear he has been doing a bang up job. So, now that you've been properly introduced I'm going to refresh my high ball, mingle with the old folks, and let you get to know each other."

I wasn't prepared to like Amber, but she had a natural way of putting people at ease with her confidence which didn't come off as arrogant or vain. She was striking, but seemed to be totally unaware of her beauty and I could certainly understand why Mrs. Bell might have had an issue with her husband spending so much time with his young protégé. She was far more interested in what I was doing that summer than talking about herself. When I told her about the trip to the waterfall and the amusement park and the camping trip she seemed to get lost in her memories of when she had been a camp counselor.

Every time I tried to turn the conversation over to what she had been doing she quickly changed the subject. *"It's not very interesting."* she told me. *"I work in the U.S Attorney's office. We prosecute criminals. Tony Bell and I have been working on a big case this summer. That's the reason neither of us have been able to spend much time here this summer. I feel sorry for his family. He can't even tell them what we're working on. We both took oaths. And if we discuss anything with anybody the whole case, everything we've been working on could fall apart. We could be disbarred. Even if I could talk about what I'm doing, I'd rather listen to you tell me about your summer. It brings back some wonderful memories. Most of my friends are getting married and starting to have families. I have a career, but I don't have a life. Being here, listening to what's been going on this summer, makes me feel young again."*

After I reassured her she was still young, Bob's next door neighbors the Winterbottoms came over to congratulate Amber on her birthday. I took that as my opportunity to leave and once we said goodbye, I made my way across the crowded patio to thank Bob for inviting me.

"Thanks for coming by," he said. *"You brought the average age down by at least fifty years. And you got to meet Amber. Isn't she the limit! She'll be back for the big bash at the end of the summer. I had a feeling you two would get along. Did you eat? Stuff a few eggrolls in your pocket. Nobody's eating. I can't stand the thought of all this fabulous food going to waste."*

There was an antique car rally at the Inn the following weekend and everywhere you looked were vintage Duesenberg's, Studebakers and Model A's. Mario Andretti, the Italian-born racing driver; one of the most successful Americans in the history of the sport, was the honored guest and he seemed to be everywhere signing autographs and posing for pictures. When I met him he asked me where I was from and told me he lived down the road in Nazareth.

Q and Karen wanted to go out that weekend, and since the Inn was swarming with car enthusiasts we decided to go bowling at the Mountainhome Bowling Center in Cresco. Julian was busy doing whatever it was he did on weekends, so I invited Veronica and she accepted.

The Bowling Center had definitely seen better days. It was loud and smelled like stale beer and pizza, just the way we liked it. After we picked up our bowling shoes, Q ordered a pitcher of *Yuengling* and two large pizzas.

Few things are better stress relievers than bowling. It's hard to be uptight when you are wearing a pair of multi-colored shoes that everyone and his brother has worn for generations. Instead of breaking furniture at home on Saturday night, you are provided with an unlimited supply of cheap beer and expected to roll heavy round balls down an ally to obliterate neatly arranged grouping of pins that look like soldiers standing at attention. What's more, it's impossible to have a serious conversation with anyone because moments after you sit down someone starts waving their arms at you telling you it's your turn again.

We bowled for just under two hours, and since the pizza had become cold and soggy, Karen suggested we go to an all-night diner on the highway across the street from one of her father's car dealerships and order Boston Cream pie.

Besecker's Diner moved to 5th street in East Stroudsburg in 1978 and was popular with the locals and tourists alike. In addition to serving breakfast all day, which I thought was an excellent idea, they were famous for their homemade soups and pies. We got there around 10:30 and slipped into a comfortable booth at the far side of the diner. A long counter ran the entire length of the diner in front of which stood round stools bolted to the linoleum floor. On top of the counter, displayed in tall glass domes approximately eight feet apart, was a tempting assortment of homemade pies and frosted layer cakes, including the Boston Cream pie that Karen had raved about. Her eyes lit up when the waitress carved an enormous wedge and placed it in front of her and Q with two forks. Veronica and I were in the mood for breakfast, so we ordered eggs over easy with bacon and drank coffee while Karen and Q devoured their pie.

We finished eating around 11:30 and when I got up to pay the bill, I noticed our waitress was twirling a curl in her hair as she gazed into the eyes of a handsome man sitting at the counter.

"So where are you going at this hour, looking so handsome?" she said in a breathy voice.

"Home" he said. *"To surprise my wife. I had a meeting nearby and it got late. Rather than drive all the way back to Philadelphia, I'm going to spend the night in Buck Hill. I have a place there and I'm looking forward to spending some time with my family."*

Disappointed, she gave him his change and he left a twenty dollar bill on the counter.

After the man left, I noticed he had left his briefcase under the counter. As quickly as I could, I grabbed it and dashed out into the parking lot, but by the time I got there all I could see was the tail lights of his Ford Bronco as it disappeared around a bend in the road.

When I got back inside, Q was standing by the front door jingling his keys.

"Where'd you go?" he asked. *"We thought you were running on the check. Look, if you're short on cash, just let me know. I'll be glad to loan you a few simoleons."*

"No, it wasn't that." I told him. *Some guy left his briefcase."* Looking for the waitress, I hoisted the heavy briefcase up onto the counter and saw a small leather tag.

"At least we'll be able to find him" I said as I fumbled with the tag. Turning it over I saw the name. *"Anthony Bell, Esquire, U.S. Attorney's Office."*

"Holy shit!" I said loud enough for everyone to hear.

"That's Briny's father! We need to go right now."

"It's a damn briefcase!" said Q as we walked out to the car. *"He won't even notice it's gone until tomorrow morning."*

"That's not it." I said. *"He's going home. Unexpectedly! Julian has been sleeping with his wife and I'm pretty sure he's there tonight! We need to warn them. How fast can this car go, without getting us killed or getting pulled over by a cop?"*

"You can't have it both ways, brother!" Q said as he turned the key in the ignition and the engine roared to life. *"But I'll do my best."*

After we hit 70 miles per hour on the road next to a river where the speed limit was 45, I began to regret what I had asked him to do. He was a good driver and I knew if something unexpected, like a deer crossed our path, he would react appropriately. Even after two pitchers of beer. As the mailboxes and telephone poles whizzed past my window with increasing speed, illuminated by the pale yellow light of our headlights, I wondered if dying in a car crash would be less painful if I relaxed and didn't tense up. At this speed I knew there was only a slim chance of surviving.

We finally passed Mr. Bell on blind curve just outside Mountainhome which was about ten minutes away from Buck Hill Falls. I held my breath as we blew by the Police Station where Michael had spent the night, and a few moments later, the blur that was Maccioni's.

The Bell's house was dark when we arrived except for a small reading lamp that had been left on in the living room. I wasn't absolutely sure Julian was there, but I knew Briny was having a sleepover at the Cullen's that night so I had a pretty strong feeling she wasn't alone. I thought about knocking on the front door, but at that point there wasn't much time. In less than a minute, Mr. Bell would be walking up the front stairs to their bedroom and see his wife in bed with someone who looked like a singer in a grunge band.

Veronica and I moved silently and quickly through the shadows cast by the moonlight that night along the side yard to the back of the house. As soon as we got there I remembered where the master bedroom was and saw that someone had left a window open and a breeze was pulling the lace curtains outside into the night air.

"*Julian!*" I whispered.

When nobody answered, I took a deep breath and shouted "*Julian!*"

With time running out, I reached down and grabbed a small stone from her garden and attempted to throw it through the open window, but missed. The sound of breaking glass was enough to wake the dead and several seconds later Julian's face appeared in the window.

"*Danny! What the hell! You broke the fucking window!*"

"*I know*" I said. "*It doesn't matter. You need to get out of there. Her husband is about to come home and he's not going to be happy finding you in bed with his wife.*"

"Are you crazy? How do you know this?"

"I know. Julian, you have to trust me."

"Okay. I just need to get dressed."

"You don't have time. Throw me your clothes."

Seconds later Julian's clothes came flying out the bedroom window and floated softly to the ground. As Veronica and I ran around gathering up his socks and underwear we saw the headlights of Mr. Bell's Bronco sweep across the lawn like prison searchlights forcing us to dive for cover behind a low boxwood hedge. After we heard the car door slam, we looked up from our hiding place and watched Julian open the bedroom window as far as it would go. It was not a large window and Julian had trouble fitting his naked body through the small opening. First came his legs followed by his butt and eventually his upper body except for his head. Beneath the window was an ivy covered trellis that Julian was trying to locate with his right foot hoping it might serve as a ladder so he wouldn't have to jump. After several failed attempts, he finally found a rung with his toe and wiggled his foot into position on the latticework. After he pushed down on it several times, to determine if it was strong enough to hold his weight, he committed to the plan and swung the rest of his body out the open window. For a moment it seemed like he was going to be able to climb down the trellis like a ladder, until we heard a terrifying cracking sound as the trellis ripped away from the side of the Bell's house and Julian plummeted from the sky like Tarzan swinging on a broken vine.

By the grace of God Julian managed to avoid landing on a small concrete statue of a cherub that Mrs. Bell had placed in the center of her prized scarlet begonia patch. We were able to find most of Julian's clothes, but there wasn't time to double check as we rushed him into Q's waiting car. Nobody said a word as we drove away, but I couldn't help but wonder what Mrs. Bell was going to say to her husband about the broken window and how she was going to explain whatever evidence had been left scattered around backyard. She seemed like a nice woman. I liked her, and I felt for her and her husband, but mostly I felt sorry for Briny.

There was an employee barbeque the last Sunday of every month during the summer and Q told me to meet him there around 6:30. He wanted to talk to me about something and said since it was for employees only, organized by employees and management had absolutely nothing to do with it, the food they served was excellent. I had missed the first two employee barbeques, so I was glad that I got to experience at least one that summer.

The barbeque was held in an open field behind the maintenance facility where the antique car show had taken place. When I arrived I saw that it had been transformed into what looked like a Medieval fairgrounds. In the middle of the field was what looked like a circus tent surrounded by picnic tables and a row of oil barrel barbeques next to a large smoker where a chef was busy pulling strips of pork off a roast pig into a sea of sweet smelling barbeque sauce. People were playing horseshoes off to the side and someone had placed different colored flags around the field so people would be able to find their friends.

Q had instructed me to meet him by the green flag and when I walked over I saw him sitting in a folding beach chair wearing dark sunglasses, a bucket hat and a Hawaiian shirt. When he saw me, he told me to grab some food and asked me to bring him another beer, if I had enough hands. Somehow I managed, and by the time I got back he had rustled up another beach chair for me to sit in. One of the Jamaican landscapers had brought a boom box and *Bob Marley* was telling everyone not to worry, but when I heard what Q had to say, I wasn't so sure.

Cause every little thing gonna be all right
Don't worry about a thing
Cause every little thing is gonna be all right...

"Right now Vinny Goombah is sitting at my desk messing with my spreadsheets. If they do an audit, those numbers are going to have my name on them, and I'm way too good-looking to spend time in prison. So to protect my ass, I made copies of everything. I taped some of their phone calls. And as an added measure of security, kind of like an insurance policy, I took Vinnie's bottle of Mr. PiBB. So if anything unusual happens to me, if I suddenly go missing, you need to find Mr. PiBB. It's in a plastic bag in the trunk of my car covered with Mr. Goombah's greasy fingerprints. What kind of a person even drinks Mr. PiBB? Bad people, that's who. People who can't be trusted. As long as there's Dr. Pepper, there's no reason for Mr. PiBB to exist!"

"I hear what you're saying" I told Q. *"And I agree with you about Mr. PiBB. But what can we do about it? This is way bigger than you or me. No offense, but we are a couple of nobody's. I'm not sure this is our battle to fight. And even if we did, I'm pretty sure we wouldn't win."*

"You're right. You and I are two farts in a hurricane. But there's a part of this you are too young to understand. As we get older, the only thing that separates one individual from another is their reputation. There are plenty of people who can do my job making columns of numbers add up. It's really not that difficult. The only thing that separates me from everybody else is my reputation. Once your reputation is blown, it's impossible to repair it. So if this blows up, and my reputation is somehow attached to it, it's going to follow me around for the rest of my life. So even if it's not our battle to fight, I guess you could say it's pretty important to me."

I liked Q, and I appreciated the fact that he trusted me, but I felt like I was being dragged in over my head. For some reason he seemed to think that I knew people who might be able to help, and maybe I did. But then again, maybe I didn't? Bob Robertson was on the board of directors of the Inn and a lawyer but the stakes were too high to ask him for help and he had proven to be unreliable. Amber was a possibility, but we had just met and she was young and I wasn't sure if it was fair to drag her into this mess. Unfortunately, the person I needed to reach out to was the man whose window I had just broken so he wouldn't walk in on my roommate who was in bed with his wife.

Before we left the barbeque that afternoon Q and I came up a plan. We would meet the next day at *The Happy Hooker Bait & Tackle Shop* in Cresco and he would hand over whatever evidence he had been able to collect. Then, it was my job to deliver the evidence to Briny's father without anyone knowing where it came from.

Julian was in bed recovering from his injuries when I got back to Cottage 16 that night. He asked how the barbeque was and I told him it was great and the food was excellent. He had some cuts on his face and arms from Mrs. Bell's Hybrid Tea Roses and his ankle was swollen, but considering what had happened he was fortunate he didn't break any bones. We still hadn't spoken about the incident and to be honest I wasn't exactly sure what to say. Briny didn't go to camp the following day, and when he didn't show up the day after that, I thought we should give his mother a call to make sure he was okay. Technically, it was Julian's responsibility to contact the parents of campers we were concerned about, but given what had happened the other night, I thought it might be better if I made the call myself. After she answered the phone I told her who was calling and asked if Briny was going to be at Camp Club that week. It took a moment for her to reply, but she finally spoke up.

"Briny's fine" she said. *"He's spending a few days with his father in Haverford. They haven't seen each other much this summer, and I needed some time to myself. Thank you for calling, Danny. I appreciate your concern. You have a good day now."* Then she hung up.

After Camp Club the next day I borrowed another abandoned bicycle that had been sitting out behind the Arts & Crafts building and peddled to *The Happy Hooker Bait and Tackle Shop* where I planned to meet Q. The place was deserted when I got there, except for a bored looking clerk who was thumbing through the pages of what looked like a 'girlie magazine'. Then I noticed a man standing in the back of the store wearing waders, a vest covered with colorful flies and a camouflage hat. At first, I thought he was a mannequin, because he hadn't moved when I entered the shop, but then I saw him adjust a wicker fishing creel hanging from a leather strap that was looped across his shoulder. Moving in for a closer look, I tapped him gently on the shoulder causing him to jump and knock over a rack of fishing poles.

"Excuse me" I said, recognizing that the fisherman was actually Q.

Before I could say another word, he held up one finger instructing me to be quiet and whispered, *"The trout on the wall is watching. See his eyes? One of them is a camera. I'm not sure which one, but we need to be careful. Just don't look at the trout."*

When we got to a corner of the store where Q felt comfortable he removed the fishing creel from his shoulder and handed it to me.

"Here, take this. Inside is everything you need. Just make sure it gets to the right person. Someone you trust. Whatever you do, don't tell them who gave it to you. Because if you do, I'm

a dead man. You might as well put a gun to my head and pull the trigger."

When he finished talking, we walked around the perimeter of the store, to avoid the watchful trout, and I bought a box of night crawlers from Bubba trying not to make eye contact as he slowly counted out my change.

As soon as I got back to the cottage, I dumped the contents of the creel out onto my bed. Inside was a Sony M-470 microcassette voice recorder, a handful of cassettes, a ledger book and two rolls of undeveloped film. It didn't look like much, but I hoped it was enough to put whoever was trying to take over the Inn in jail for a long time. When I heard someone coming up the stairs, I shoved everything back inside the creel and pushed it under my bed.

"*How's it going?*" Julian asked standing in the doorway to my bedroom.

"*Pretty good*" I said. "*Far as I can tell.*"

For a moment he just stood there looking at me like he wanted to say something, but wasn't sure where to begin.

"*I want to apologize for the other night. It wasn't my finest hour. I have no idea how you got dragged into it, but it was never my intention for you to get involved. It's a bit complicated, which doesn't make it right, but there are a few things that you should probably know. Libby and her husband have been living separate lives for more than a year. Her husband has buried himself in his work. She's trying to figure out her next move. Briny doesn't know a thing about it, just that his father has been spending a lot of time at the office. They were trying to work things out, but after what happened the other night, I'm not sure that's possible."*

"Where does that leave you?" I asked.

"I'm just a place holder. Things that are temporary, that aren't meant to last, are often more intriguing than things we are familiar with. Like cut flowers, or a Christmas tree that you cherish until the season is over and then it gets tossed aside. Women like Libby don't stay with men like me for very long. It's also possible that she has been using me to get back at her inattentive husband. Now that the 'bloom is off the rose', things between us will never be the same. I just felt like you deserved some kind of an explanation."

While I was trying to figure out the best way to get in touch with Mr. Bell, I thought about contacting the FBI directly and even looked up their phone number which I found out is 1-800-CALL-FBI. Then, I tried to imagine what the special agent who answered the phone would say to his or her field officer about a camp counselor calling from the Poconos to report the possible illegitimate acquisition of the Buck Hill Falls Inn by the mafia. I was pretty sure the first question they would ask me was how I had obtained the evidence, followed by the name and contact information of the person who had given it to me. What seemed to be the safest option was to hand the evidence over to Mr. Bell and let the U.S. Attorney's office handle everything.

The last campers were usually picked up by their parents or a nanny around 4:15, so it was impossible for me to leave Buck Hill Falls and get to Mr. Bell's office in Philadelphia before 6:45 when he would probably be just sitting down to dinner with Briny in Haverford. The last thing Briny needed was for his camp counselor to show up unexpectedly at his house at night asking to speak to his father about another thing his father would have a hard time explaining. The best option seemed to be to go to their house at night after Briny had gone to bed.

The next thing I needed to figure out was where the Bell's lived when they weren't at Buck Hill; which was easy because there was an address book with everyone's home address in Julian's desk at Camp Club, and how I was going to get there. Veronica never let anyone drive her car and if I asked if I could borrow it she would want to know where I was going and I wasn't prepared to tell her. The way I looked at it, the fewer people who knew what I was up to, the better. I knew it was against the rules, but the only option I had was to borrow the SS Groovy from the maintenance facility and try to return her before anyone noticed she was gone. The keys were in Julian's desk drawer, with the address book, so when I broke into the Camp Club building that night after it got dark I would be able pick up both at the same time.

As soon as I was able to convince myself I was doing the right thing, I went back to my bedroom and reached under the bed to locate the fishing creel and lifted the lid to make sure everything Q had handed me was still there. Thankfully, it was. I suppose I was getting a little paranoid because when I cut through the woods behind Cottage 16 on the way to Camp Club I had a strange feeling I was being watched. Back in the shadows, behind a tree, I thought I saw the glow of a cigarette and even though hotel guests occasionally wandered off into the woods to sneak a smoke, they rarely ventured out more than twenty feet from the putting green.

My heart raced when I got to Camp Club, which seemed much scarier at night when nobody was there. I tried to open the front door, which I knew would be locked, and after my suspicions were confirmed, I went around to each of the six windows on the sides of the building to see if any had been left open. Fortunately, the last window I tried to open slid up easily and I was able to hoist myself inside the building without anyone seeing me. Quick as a cat, I wrote down the Bell's address, grabbed the keys to the bus and slipped out into the night through the open window.

It was probably my imagination, but it felt like the SS Groovy was happy to see me. We hadn't gone on many adventures lately and the engine roared to life as soon as I turned the key in the ignition. As we drove past the gate of the maintenance facility parking lot it felt good to finally be doing something, rather than just thinking about it. Once we got onto the highway I pushed the SS Groovy about as fast as she would go heading toward 27 Morning Dove Lane.

As I drove I started to think about what I was going to say to Briny's father after I rang the doorbell, and I hoped he wouldn't recognize me from the diner where he had left his briefcase a few nights ago. I didn't remember making eye contact with him as the waitress was busy chatting him up, but at one point we were standing shoulder to shoulder at the counter.

Haverford is an affluent township 3 miles west of Philadelphia in an area referred to as the "Main Line" which goes back to a time when the Pennsylvania Railroad added local stops to a string of backwater towns west of the city that helped turn them into fashionable suburbs. The Bells lived in a beautiful colonial home in a wooded area with manicured lawns, tall hedges and pebble driveways that made a pleasant crunching sound as you walked or drove on them. The only vehicle that could have looked more conspicuous would have been a Mexican Taco truck designed to look like a giant sombrero. Just down the street from the Bell's house was a construction site where I parked the SS Groovy behind a dumpster. It wasn't ideal, but there weren't many options. After I turned the engine off, I grabbed the fishing creel and walked across the muddy lot and down the street toward the Bell's house.

It's rarely good news when someone rings your doorbell late at night and that evening was no exception. As I walked up the Bell's driveway and turned left onto the brick path that led to their front door, I considered leaving the evidence on the front porch and giving him a call at the office the next morning to explain. However, when I was halfway along the path I must have triggered a motion sensor because an array of lights suddenly flicked on and the entire front yard was bathed in bright floodlights. I froze in my tracks when I saw a light go on upstairs. My heart was pounding so hard I thought it might come out of my chest as I stood in front of the house gripping the fishing creel and waited for Mr. Bell to come to the door.

"Is there something I can help you with?" said Mr. Bell after he opened the door a crack.

"I'm Daniel Barnes" I said. *"From Buck Hill Falls. I'm Briny's camp counselor."*

"Briny won't be at camp this week. He's staying with me. Is something wrong?

"No. I'm not here about Briny. I need to talk to you about something else. Would it be okay if I came inside for a few minutes, so I can try to explain."

"It's late, and I just finished putting Briny to bed, but if you came all this way, it must be important, so come on in. But we need to talk quietly, because I don't want to wake him up."

After I unlaced my muddy hiking boots and left them by the front door, he walked me into their living room and motioned for me to take a seat on the couch.

"Can I get you anything? Maybe a glass of water?"

After I thanked him for the offer and told him I was fine, he noticed the fishing creel and gave me a puzzled look. *"A little late in the evening for fishing, isn't it son?"*

"Yes sir. I can explain. A friend of mine, someone I met at the beginning of the summer at the Inn works in accounting and is very concerned about some things that have been going on there. Illegal things. As well as some bad people who have been hanging around the office. My friend is a little paranoid, but I don't believe he is crazy. He got knocked unconscious a week ago and he's worried about his safety, and his reputation and what might happen if these people take over the Inn and turn it into a

gambling destination. He isn't sure who to trust but he has a bad feeling about what's going on and he thinks the families who live there, the Cottagers and maybe even the FBI should know about it. But nobody seems to be paying attention"

"That's quite a story son." Mr. Bell said. *"So what's in the fishing basket?"*

"Evidence sir. That my friend collected. Proof that what's going on is illegal."

"Would you mind opening it? So I can see what's inside." he said eyeing the creel as if it might contain a venomous snake.

"Sure", I said, as I removed the ivory peg from the lid and tilted it towards him.

"From what I can see, there appears to be a ledger book, and some tapes, and a few rolls of film. Is that everything? What's on the tapes?" he asked.

"I have no idea. Conversations? I haven't listened to them or even looked at the ledger. Even if I did, I would have no idea what I was looking for. I'm just the messenger for my friend who wants to remain anonymous. If anyone finds out, he's convinced somebody will kill him."

Mr. Bell didn't make any promises that night, but he told me to leave the creel on the coffee table where it was sitting and said he would examine the evidence in the morning and see if my story made any sense. Before we said goodbye, I thanked him for listening and he told me he was planning to bring Briny back to Camp Club that weekend. *"Maybe we'll go fishing."* he said trying lighten the mood a little before I headed back to Buck Hill Falls.

You can only imagine the tremendous sense of relief I felt when I climbed behind the wheel of the SS Groovy and backed out of the muddy construction site. I wasn't sure if Mr. Bell recognized me from the diner the other night because his face, although handsome, remained expressionless the entire time I was there. I imagined he would have been a good poker player because he didn't react to anything I said, even when I told him my friend had been knocked unconscious. Most people I knew would have made a face or at least cringed. I guess that was a good trait for an attorney to have, but I understood how it might have driven his wife mad.

I didn't get back to Buck Hill Falls until 1:30 in the morning and turned the headlights off when I rolled as quietly as possible past the Camp Club building and made a sharp left turn into the parking lot behind the maintenance facility. Then I pocketed the keys and planned to return them to Julian's desk drawer the next day after our staff meeting when nobody was looking. I decided to take the long way home following the road rather than take the shortcut through the dark patch of woods behind Cottage 16 where earlier I had sensed someone watching me. After I climbed the creaky winding staircase I fell asleep the moment my head hit the pillow.

Every summer has a beginning, a middle and an end. When I was in high school the beginning of summer was usually filled with making plans and hopeful anticipation of being able to spend time outdoors with my friends doing the things we wanted to do, rather than the things we had to do. The days grew longer in the middle of summer and time seemed to slow to a standstill as we sat in the warm sunshine by the lake or I listened to baseball games on my transistor radio while pulling weeds from my mother's garden. And then, all of a sudden we woke up one morning and it was the end of August and the days were getting shorter and we could feel summer slipping away like sand in an hourglass.

I woke up early on Friday and decided to go for a run before our morning staff meeting to clear my head. So much had been going on recently that I couldn't think straight. Since I was a freshman in high school, going for a run had always been my escape route from things I had no control over. Once I found my stride and my breathing became regular my problems seemed to melt away and the questions that had been swirling around in my head answered themselves. My friends had accused me of running away from my problems and I guess, in a way, they were right.

The morning air was cool and fresh and as I ran past the lawn bowling courts I could sense September approaching like a faraway train. Families were beginning to pack up their station wagons and head home for the first day of school while older versions of themselves were returning to the Poconos for the autumn season and discounted room rates. It seemed like overnight the roads had become littered with acorns, and even though the leaves had not yet started to turn yellow you could tell they were starting to think about it.

As I ran past the girls cottage, I thought I saw Veronica in her upstairs bedroom window getting ready for our last day of camp and I suddenly realized how much I was going to miss her. We had been together on daily basis since the beginning of June and our relationship had come full circle. If Julian hadn't twisted our fates together as co-counselors we would never have had the opportunity to spend so much time together. We would have been friends, but I doubt we would have shared so many of our innermost thoughts and secrets that eventually led to us falling in love. If we had not become lovers, that side of Veronica would have always remained a mystery to me and even though our romantic relationship had lasted less than three months, I knew I would never forget or regret the times that we spent together. Even after she apologized and told me that she had lied to me and then dumped me, I was still in love with her. There was no way of knowing what the future would bring, but now that summer was coming to a close I was gradually accepting the fact that we would always be just friends.

The Buck Hill Bounce took place every Labor Day Weekend to celebrate the end of the summer and the beginning of Fall. In order to get an invitation you had to be a dues paying member in good standing of the *Lot and Cot*, because they were the ones who covered the costs of the evening, but Bob Robertson had insisted that Amber and I join him as his guests.

The Bounce, as it was commonly referred to by the members, was one of the few parties of the season where women could get dressed up and the men traditionally wore blue blazers and colorful bow ties. I'd always thought bow ties looked ridiculous on anyone except young children and old men, but Bob assured me that was not the case.

"Nonsense. Women love bow ties. It's a James Bond thing."

When I told him I didn't own a bow tie and had no idea how to tie one, Bob said to stop by his cottage on the way to the party and he would be glad to loan me one of his.

Q drove past the playground outside of Camp Club on his way home from work on Friday afternoon and leaned out the window to ask me how things had gone with my contact in the District Attorneys' office. He didn't get out of his car but he breathed a noticeable sigh of relief when I told him that I thought things had gone really well, even though I wasn't exactly sure how things had gone. Before he drove off he asked if I wanted to join him at Johnnie Diamonds for happy hour, but I told him I was busy even though I didn't have any plans.

I was glad I turned him down because when I got back to Cottage 16 Julian said he was ordering Chinese food, and since we hadn't had a meal together all summer, he said it was time for us to "*break bread.*" After the food arrived Julian set up candles around the room and we sat cross legged on the living room floor and ate with chopsticks from cardboard takeout containers.

"*I want to apologize for not being a better roommate.*" Julian said. "*I wasn't around much. But it seemed to have worked out. Part of being a good roommate, I've learned, is not getting too involved in the other person's business. I thought you handled the Veronica thing pretty well, considering. And you stuck your neck out for me at the Bell's house the other night. That was brave. And probably stupid. On both our parts. Have you tried the Moo Shu pork? It's amazing! So what do you think you'll do next year? Are you considering coming back?*"

When I told him I wasn't sure he nodded his head and said *"That's an honest answer. None of us can be sure about anything. Things can turn on a dime, and they often due. Buck Hill is a pretty small community and I'm pretty sure I won't be asked back next year. But I would be glad to put in a good word for you, if you want to come back. Next summer will be completely different. We never step into the same river twice Danny, because the river is always changing."*

After we finished eating dinner, Julian asked me if I wanted to get high and I told him I appreciated his offer but I didn't think weed was my thing and I needed to get some rest.

"Suit yourself" he said as he filled his water pipe with a plug of Humboldt's finest.

I slept late on Saturday and walked over to the maintenance facility to do some laundry so I would have a clean shirt to wear to the party that evening. On the way, I cut through the woods and walked past the spot where I thought I had seen someone smoking in the shadows the other night. Sure enough, next to a fallen tree was a circle of *Virginia Slims* cigarette butts and a single gold hoop earring. I was relieved to discover what had probably been going on that night was more along the lines of a romantic encounter rather than a mafia hit man intent on intercepting the evidence Q had given me that I was taking to the U.S District Attorney's office.

I borrowed an iron from Veronica on the way home and after I had done my best to get the wrinkles out of my only white button down shirt, I slipped on my blue blazer and walked over to Bob's Cottage. Before I was able to knock on the door, he greeted me and handed me a gin and tonic in one of his oversized glasses.

"Amber called and said she's running late so she'll meet us at the party" Bob said as he escorted me by the elbow to his living room where he had spread out at least thirty bow ties of all colors, shapes and sizes. Most were too outrageous for me to wear, but I picked out classy-looking orange and black tie, similar to one he told me my father had worn at Princeton and we practiced tying them in front of the full length mirror in his front foyer.

After we were satisfied with the shape of our bow ties, we walked outside and joined the "March of the Penguins" on their way to the tennis veranda where the event was being held.

On the way over Bob announced that the three of us would be sitting at a table with Mr. and Mrs Bell and my father's ex-wife, Darlene Fitzpatrick, whom he said I would be meeting with the following week when my father's estate was being settled. *"I thought this would be a good opportunity for you to get to know each other"* Bob explained.

As usual, Bob's intentions were good, but I felt the blood drain out of my face when I suddenly realized this was going to be one of the most awkward evenings of my entire life.

Amber was sitting at the table when we arrived wearing a red sequin dress that made her look more like a movie star than a prosecutor. She stood up when we got there and smiled. *"I was hoping I wasn't going to have the whole table all to myself"* she said.

Bob greeted her with a kiss on the cheek and said. *"That would never happen my dear. And even if it did, the way you look tonight this table would be full of adoring young men. You remember Danny. He was just hanging around, so I asked him to join us."*

Bob made a beeline to the bar so I sat down next to Amber and told her I liked her dress and said I was glad she was able to join us so I would have someone to talk to. She seemed to appreciate the compliment and told me she liked my bow tie.

"First time I've ever worn one. Bob helped me tie it. Are the two sides even?" I asked.

"Almost" she said as she straightened one of the sides *"Pretty good for your first time. So I heard you were in the neighborhood. You should have called. My place isn't far from there."*

When I didn't say anything she put her hand on my shoulder and told me not to worry. *"Tony and I are a team. We're on it. Something's going to happen. We're just not sure when."*

Several minutes later Bob returned from the bar, with a drink in each hand, and a tall blond woman clutching to his left arm. When they arrived at the table where Amber and I were sitting he set down his drinks and introduced me to my father's ex-wife.

"Danny, I'd like to introduce you to Darlene Fitzpatrick who was married to your father before he met your mother. Darlene lives in Texas now, but she comes back to Buck Hill, like the swallows to Capistrano, every summer to visit. I thought it would be nice for you two to get to know each other socially before our meeting next week to settle your father's estate."

"Pleasure to meet you Danny" she says, extending her diamond encrusted hand. *"But it feels like we might have met somewhere before. Not just because you have your father's eyes. Something else. Wait, I remember. We met at the Inn when Winkie had that accident. We both felt just terrible. He's usually such a good boy. I hope you are able to forgive us?"*

After I reassured her that getting peed on by her diabetic dog was not the worst thing that had happened to me that day, leaving out the part about my girlfriend dropping me like a jelly doughnut with a bug on it earlier that morning, she asked me how my summer was going.

"It's been great" I told her. *"I've met some interesting people and I've done a lot of interesting things that I probably wouldn't have been able to do, thanks to Bob."*

"Well, Bob and I go back a long time. He and your father were great friends. It's unfortunate you never got to meet your father. He had many good qualities. And from what I've heard, you seemed to have inherited quite a few of your father's good graces. But I guess we will see when we have our little meeting next week. If you passed the test, or not."

I wasn't sure what she was referring to when she mentioned the word "test". Had my summer at Buck Hill been some kind of a test I was required to pass in order to receive my inheritance? When I first met Bob, he mentioned something called a 'morals clause' but he had assured me that it was merely a technicality. I admit, some pretty unusual things had gone on that summer, but I was pretty confident that none of them would disqualify me from inheriting whatever money I deserved from my father that would help pay my college tuition.

From the looks on both of their faces, Bob had not told the Bell's that Amber and I would be joining them at his table for dinner that night. It was pretty obvious Mrs. Bell blamed Amber for her husband's absence that summer and was sure that the two of them had been shacking up in hotel rooms all over town. Amber did her best to connect with Mrs. Bell in hopes of convincing her that wasn't true, but her low cut, tight fitting sequin dress wasn't helping.

Mr. Bell was understandably perplexed when he saw me sitting at the table with Amber sipping a rum punch with a pink umbrella that Bob had just brought over. When Bob introduced us and told him I was Briny's camp counselor, we both acted like we had never met.

As soon as we could slip away, Amber and I excused ourselves and walked over to the bar that was farthest away from our table and she ordered two shots of tequila with lime.

"*Well, that couldn't have been more awkward*" she said as we clinked our glasses and downed our shots. "*I love my uncle Bob, but I sometimes wonder how he got into Princeton. If her eyes could kill, I'd be dead. That woman is convinced I'm having an affair with her husband. That I'm the reason he's been working so hard and hasn't been here all summer. Whatever is going on between them has nothing to do with me. If she only knew what we've really been doing, she might cut him some slack. It's important. Not more important than spending time with his family, but that's his business. Then The U.S. Attorney witnesses his key informant sitting at his table sipping a Pina colada. Small world, wouldn't you say? And the frosting on the cake is you get introduced to your "ex-step whatever in-law" for the first time, or the second if we are going to count the "wee-wee incident", at the Buck Hill Bounce. Honestly, and I hope you don't mind me saying this, but she looks like she just stepped out of an episode of Dallas.*

As soon as the Motown band began to play *"It's the same old song"* by *The Four Tops* Amber hopped up and down like a giddy teenager and said *"Hey, I love this song! I know I'm a lot older than you, but would you mind dancing with me? Just this one song."*

We ended up returning to the table only once to eat dinner, and Amber taught me some new dance moves that I was able to quickly assimilate into my limited repertory of things I felt comfortable doing on a crowded dance floor. More than once, while were dancing, I caught Mr. and Mrs. Bell looking over at us as if they were trying to figure out who knew what and how long whatever it was we knew would remain a secret. As for my father's ex-wife, she seemed to be watching our every move and danced a few songs with Bob, but left the party early without saying goodbye after he danced with someone else and she had to sit out a few songs.

The Sunday of Labor Day weekend at Buck Hill Falls, and most other seasonal resorts, was a day of transition. As their parents packed up the family car, I noticed the kids noses were buried in the book they were supposed to have read before going back to school. Veronica and I spent most of the weekend hanging around the Camp Club building with the other counselors so we could say goodbye to our campers as they made their way back home. It was Veronica's idea to park the SS Groovy out front with a sign that said "SEE YOU NEXT YEAR!"

To accommodate everyone's schedules, Bob had moved our estate settlement meeting to Monday, which was technically a holiday, but nobody seemed to mind. He said had reserved the executive boardroom on the second floor of the Inn for our meeting and told me not to eat breakfast because he had ordered pastries and a fruit platter from the main dining room. My mom was going to pick me up the following day after she got off work, and I didn't have much to pack so after Veronica and I said goodbye to the last two campers, I asked if she wanted to go for a celebratory swim in the pool before we went our separate ways and she said yes.

The lifeguards had gone home for the day and the gate to the pool was locked, so we hopped the chain link fence and dove into the deep end of the pool that had finally become warm and welcoming. It was magical being alone with Veronica in the warm water as the late afternoon sunlight filtered through the branches of pine trees. The distance between us was still there, but in the space between there was a feeling of trust and understanding that could only be explained as love. Up until that point I knew I loved her, but I hadn't known for sure that she truly loved me. Our shared mutual experiences, our ups and downs, had brought us together and we both knew, or at least hoped, the bond that we shared would last forever.

I woke up early on Monday morning and ignored what Bob had said about not eating breakfast and went to dining room and ordered my usual; two eggs over easy, crisp bacon and a grilled English muffin with grape jelly. It was going to be a long day and I wanted to make sure I was well fed. Sitting at the table at the far end of the dining room was a group of men wearing dark suits surrounded by large briefcases. And drinking coffee at the other end of the room were two uniformed policemen from the Mountainhome police department and what looked like two detectives. Not the usual crowd for Labor Day Weekend in the Poconos.

After I finished my breakfast I saw Bob Robertson stride into the lobby wearing a green golf shirt and canary yellow pants. As he walked past the dining room, one of the men in dark suits recognized him and waved him over to their table.

"Bob!" the man said. *"Nice of you to get dressed up for our meeting. What time is the Easter egg hunt?"* After they shared a good laugh, Bob replied.

"It wasn't my idea to have our meeting take place during the club championship. I've accommodated you Arthur, so don't give me a hard time. In fact you look a bit pale for the end of the summer. You should try to get outside more. You're beginning to look like a vampire. Take up tennis. Or gardening. All those fraudulent personal injury cases seem to have sucked the life out of you. I'm hoping we can keep things civil this morning, so I can make my 12:00 tee time."

As soon as Bob saw me sitting by myself he came over and asked me how my breakfast was and after I paid we took the elevator to the second floor and walked across the hallway to the executive boardroom. It was a beautiful wood paneled room with a large mahogany table in the center surrounded by at least a dozen comfortable green leather armchairs. Before we went in, Bob introduced me to Arthur King who he said was representing my father's ex-wife.

"Daniel, let me take a moment to introduce you to Mrs Fitzpatrick's counsel Arthur King and what must be the Knights of the Round table. Arthur, this young man is Daniel Barnes."

After we shook hands we stepped into the board room where we saw Mrs. Fitzpatrick sitting at the far end of the room next to a woman who was wearing a dark blue pants suit and tortoise shell glasses and looked a lot like Mrs. Burdler the tour guide. She was holding a long, thin cigarette and on the table next to her was a fresh pack of *Virginia Slims.* Unlike the other night where she had been all smiles, Mrs. Fitzpatrick looked like she was ready for battle.

Once Bob finished pouring himself a large cup of black coffee he stood at the head of the table and addressed the group.

"Well, it's a pleasure to see everyone here this morning. To be honest, I'm not sure why some of you are here but I'm going to assume Darlene invited you for a reason. I'm glad to finally be able to wrap up this matter, which I think we all agree, has gone on for far too long. Since I have already reviewed the terms of my close friend's last will and testament with his intended recipients, and everyone is in agreement with the terms outlined in that document, there's really no need for me to go page by page

through the lengthy legalese, which is mostly boilerplate, but if you have any questions now would be a good time to ask them."

When nobody indicated that they had a question, Bob continued.

"As most of us are aware, my deceased client, this young man's father, God rest his soul, was a very moral man who lived his life to higher standards than most of us can even aspire to. And, as he so clearly outlined in these documents, he wanted those values to be reflected in whatever he passed along to his intended heirs. Any violation of the terms of the agreement, he insisted, would result in a forfeiture of the inheritance, which would be distributed either to the other intended recipient or a charity of that persons choosing."

"Since Mrs. Fitzpatrick and I have known each other for the greater part of thirty years, and I met with Mr. Barnes just a few months ago, I decided to bring him into the fold and helped him get a job here at Camp Club where I could keep a close eye on him and according to his boss and mentor Julian Snow, he has performed his duties flawlessly. So if there are no objections, I am prepared to attest to his high moral character and proceed with

the distribution of the remainder of my client's estate so I won't be late for my aforementioned 12:00 tee time."

After a moment of awkward silence, one of the younger lawyers whispered something to Arthur King who whispered something to Mrs. Fitzpatrick who whispered something to Mrs. Burdler who stood up clutching a manila envelope.

"Mrs. Burdler." said Bob. *"I'm sorry, but I'm not aware of your first name. It looks like you have something you want to present to the group. If that is the case, I urge you to proceed."*

For a woman who seemed to be talking non-stop since the day I first arrived at Buck Hill, the woman who never shut up was strangely silent.

"Mrs. Burdler?" Bob questioned. *"Do you, or do you not, have something to tell us?"*

When words refused to come from her mouth, Mr. King stood up and said, *"Thank you, Carrie. You may be seated."* Clearing his throat, he addressed the group.

"Well Bob, my client and I wish to thank you for taking this young man under your wing. It was certainly a nice thing for you to do, giving a young person an opportunity rise above his unfortunate circumstances and enjoy some of the many pleasures

a place like Buck Hill Falls has to offer. Your trust is indeed admirable. However, it has come to our attention that the person sitting to your left is not the person you seem to think he is."

"In fact, we have gathered compelling evidence that he has repeatedly broken the law, stolen property, disturbed the peace and engaged in questionable behavior of a sexual nature that is quite frankly, given the modest history of this Quaker resort, deeply disturbing. Before I show you these pictures, I must warn you that some of them are graphic in nature."

The first picture he pulled out of the envelope was of me drinking a beer with Q at Johnnie Diamonds when I first arrived. The next photo was a close up of my driver's license indicating I was underage. When Bob looked at the picture he shrugged and told Arthur to get on with it. The next series of pictures were of me and Julian smoking weed on the third floor balcony of Cottage 16. Whoever took it must have been standing on the roof of the Inn.

"Could easily have been tobacco." Bob commented. *"Plenty of people in the Middle East smoke tobacco from water pipes. There is no way to prove what they were doing was illegal."*

Reaching into his briefcase Arthur pulled out the bag of weed that was in the picture.

"So this young man smoked a little weed. Who hasn't? Even someone as old and boring as you Arthur, must have smoked weed at least once or twice when they were young. Assuming you once were young. Or maybe you were born old? Ever since I've known you, which is almost 40 years, you've been miserable and decrepit. What else have you got in there?"

"Patience, Bob. We're not here to talk about me. We're here to attest to the moral fiber of the young man sitting to your left. Which brings me to the next exhibit, which took place less than two weeks ago. As these photographs from the police report will attest, Mr. Barnes was involved in a brawl in the parking lot of a family restaurant which had to be broken up by two employees and the police. After the two men were pried apart, and their wounds attended to, one of the men involved in the brawl had to spend the night in jail. Since the person was of Asian descent, we're looking into the possibility that the brawl might have been racially motivated."

"You can't be serious!" Bob said. *"Playing the racism card in a trust settlement! If we were in front of a judge, I would motion*

to have you disbarred! I have no idea what happened that night but I'm sure Danny has a perfectly good explanation for what took place."

"I'm sorry you're offended Bob. I never said this young man was a racist. I said we are looking into several possibilities about what might have caused his violent outburst, and we are merely trying to eliminate the possibility of deep seated underlying racism."

"Okay Arthur. What else have you got? After Danny and I have an opportunity to talk about what happened that night, I will call my friends in the Mountainhome police department and hear what they have to say. How else do you plan to sully this young man's reputation?"

"A man's reputation cannot be sullied by anyone other than himself. That's the thing about reputations. We own them. Like our shadows, or prison tattoos. Our reputations are preordained by the choices that we make in life and the consequences of those choices."

"Okay, Arthur. Enough of your philosophizing. Whatever else you've got, let's see it."

"To be perfectly honest Bob, when I first saw these pictures, I wasn't sure what to make of them. Your guess is as good as mine about what might be going on here, but I thought you should see them and let everyone come to their own conclusions."

Reaching into the his briefcase, Arthur pulled out another folder with several large black and white photographs of Danny at the Pocono playhouse.

"I believe the play that night was Mousetrap, but I'm fairly certain what this young man was staring at that evening was not a mouse."

After looking at the photographs and shaking his head, Arthur King slid the pictures across the table where they came to a stop in front of Bob Robertson and me. In one of them it looks like I'm staring lecherously at the partially exposed breasts of the elderly woman sitting next to me as she attempts to cover up. In the next photo she appears to be slapping my hand as if I might have had just propositioned or groped her.

Unable to sit there any longer, I shouted, *"That was not what was happening! She was exposing herself to me. I tried to get her to stop but she wouldn't."*

After a moment Arthur said, "*Young man, I'm going to give you the benefit of the doubt on this one. None of us could figure out what was happening here. The only possible explanation any of us could come up with was you might have some kind of a 'grandmother thing' that could have happened when you were very young. Who knows, you might not even be aware you have it, but you might want to talk to a therapist. Do a little digging. See if you can work it out before whatever thoughts are going on here turn into actions.*"

"*To be completely honest we weren't even going to show you those pictures, until we received a second set of photographs from a good friend of mine who owns a home security business in the area. The other night, one of his customers was awakened late at night by the sound of breaking glass. At the same time a motion sensor in his backyard activated a camera on his garage that took pictures of what appears to be a peeping Tom or a burglar roaming the neighborhood. The pictures are a bit grainy but I think you will agree that the peeping Tom or Burglar in question bears a striking resemblance to the young man sitting on your left.*"

Needless to say it was pretty obvious that the person in question was me. I wondered why there were no pictures of Veronica or a naked man falling out of the Bell's second story window, because I'm sure they would have been included in the security footage. But clearly the only person they were interested in disparaging was me. The attack on my character had been so swift and unexpected that I didn't know where to begin to try to defend myself. I was completely and utterly overwhelmed. Finally, Bob attempted to come to my rescue.

"Well, I must admit, in all my years of practicing law I've never seen a more impressive bit of detective work. And Bravo Mrs. Burdler! From the perspective of some of these pictures, you must have climbed on top of the air conditioning units on the roof of the Inn. It's a wonder you didn't break a heel. If your ghost tours are anywhere near as intriguing as your detective work, I might have to finally go on one. Before we give Danny an opportunity to comment on these accusations, I want to point out that some of these photographs appear to have been doctored in some way. I really don't know. But my point is the images you've shown us today could easily have been altered or fabricated to tell a story rather than to present the truth. So. Unless you have

anything further to show us, I think this young man deserves an opportunity to think about what you've shown us and defend himself from these heinous accusations. Before we adjourn, Danny, is there anything you want to say?"

Caught like a deer in headlights, I looked at the pictures scattered across the table and tried to figure out where to begin. After the silence became unbearable, Bob tried to comfort me and put his hand on my shoulder. When the words still didn't come, Bob said *"You don't have to comment at this time. We can talk privately and get back to them at a later date."*

"No" I finally replied. *"I have something to say. Those pictures are real. But the story you are implying is a fabricated lie. I can explain, tell you what was really going on, but I'm not going to. Because people who trusted me would get hurt. What you are doing, how you have twisted the truth is immoral! And to hold me to a ridiculous moral standard that nobody in this room is capable of living up to is complete hypocrisy. You should be ashamed of yourselves. I'm sorry I lost my cool, but I was never that cool to begin with. And since you worked so hard to point it out, I admit that I'm not perfect. None of us are. Some of us just seem to be a little more imperfect than others. So do whatever you*

want with the money. Give it to her. Donate it to charity. Shove it up your ass if you want to. Because I don't give a damn what you do with it. I'll figure out a way to pay for college. If I learned one thing this summer, thanks to you Bob, is how to take care of myself. Because the only thing most people seem to care about is themselves."

Nobody said a word when I was done telling them what I thought of them, so I pushed my chair gently back under the table and walked quietly out of the room. When I got to the hallway, my heart was pounding and I felt like I was having a panic attack. The last thing I wanted to do was get stuck in the elevator with a bunch of people I didn't know, so I walked over to the staircase figuring I would go back to Cottage 16, pack my clothes and wait for my mother to pick me up later that afternoon. Whatever had come out of my mouth in the board room had been just as much a surprise to me as it had been to everyone else. So much had happened recently, with Veronica and what was going on with Q and the Inn, that the dam I had built to hold back all those emotions gave way and once it broke there was no stopping the feelings from flowing.

As I walked down the staircase, the two policemen and the undercover detectives from breakfast were moving quickly up the stairs in the opposite direction. One of the officers had a small microphone attached to his shoulder and I watched him lean into it and say. *"10-4, OCU. Stairway secured."* They barely even saw me as they rushed up the stairs two steps at a time and from the looks on their faces something important was about to happen.

When I got to the lobby downstairs, I noticed it had been cleared of people and two men with a German Shepard on a leash were blocking the entryway. As soon as they saw me, one of them motioned for me to step aside, and once I did the elevator doors opened and I saw two FBI agents escorting the General Manager, who had been handcuffed, into the lobby and out of the building where they helped him into the backseat of waiting Suburban. After they drove off, Mr. Bell and Amber emerged from the other elevator wearing black bulletproof vests. Even though they both saw me, neither one said hello or even acknowledged my presence.

After they drove away, I walked back to cottage 16 to pack up my belongings. It didn't take long. After I finished packing,

I peeled the tape off the picture of my mother that was on the bathroom mirror and placed it inside a book that Julian had given me. Looking around the room, I decided it was time to say goodbye to Julian so I knocked on his bedroom door. When nobody answered, I pushed the door open and saw that his room was completely empty. Even though Cottage 16 had felt very much like home that summer, after Julian left it became just another tired old building about to go into hibernation for the winter after which a new group of Camp Club employees would take our place. Wondering why he hadn't said goodbye, I grabbed my duffel bag and pillow and walked down to Camp Club to try to find Veronica.

When I got to the playground I saw Briny shooting baskets while his mother sat on the picnic table where we often had our lunch. It was just the two of them and she was wearing the bright yellow Camp Club tee shirt that Julian had given her on the first day of camp.

"Hi Danny" she said. *"I'm sorry I was rude to you on the phone. I was having a bad day when you called. And what a surprise to see you at the Lot and Cot party. I hadn't realized you and Bob Robertson were such good friends. Or that he had*

known your father. I'm sorry about what happened. It must have been rough growing up without him being around."

"We're waiting for my husband. Tony finally told me what he had been working on all summer. I'm not sure I forgive him, but I'm able to understand a little better now. And Amber seems like a nice young woman. You two looked like you had some fun on the dance floor. You helped me remember what it felt like to be young and carefree. Enjoy it. It doesn't last forever."

After she seemed to have said everything she wanted to say, I told her how much I had enjoyed being Briny's camp counselor and said I hoped he had a good year at school. When he heard me mention his name he stopped shooting baskets and walked over.

"What are you guys talking about?" he asked. *"I heard my name."*

"Nothing honey" she said. *"Danny was telling me how much fun you two had."*

"It was fun." Briny said. *"But it's sad. Why do things have to end?"*

"So something new can begin." she said trying to reassure him. *"You're looking forward to fifth grade. When I was in fifth*

grade I didn't think my life could possibly get any better, but then it did. And it kept on getting better every year after that. And next summer, when we come back, maybe Danny will be your camp counselor again. Isn't that right Danny?"

"I can't say for sure, but I'd like to come back if they'll have me". Suddenly I remembered something that I had wanted to give Briny before he left.

"Hang on a minute" I said as I walked back to my duffel bag and rummaged around the insides searching for a small white envelope that my mother had sent me a few weeks earlier.

"I have something for you. Something we talked about. I just have to find it."

Finally I found the envelope I was searching for and had him guess what was inside.

"An arrowhead? We talked about arrowheads."

"Good guess. But it's not an arrowhead."

"A coin? It looks like a coin envelope."

"Correct. But not just any coin. It's a special coin. Open it."

"Wow!" he said. *"You remembered. I don't have this one."*

Inside was a 1943 steel head Lincoln cent in mint condition from my coin collection.

"It's good luck" I said. *"It brought me good luck and now it will bring you good luck."*

After we high fived, his father walked down the hill from the Inn still wearing his bulletproof vest. As soon as he saw us he waved to his wife and the two of them began to make their way to his dark green Ford Bronco that was packed for the drive back to Haverford. When he saw me standing off to the side he came over and extended his hand.

"Thanks for keeping an eye on Briny this summer. He had a great time and Libby and I appreciate all you did for him. It was an unusual summer. They're not all like this. Thank God. But I hope we will see you next year. Oh, and thanks for the fishing tackle. Amber and I had a pretty strong case, but you helped us answer a few questions we weren't sure about. Tell your source he doesn't have to worry. We pinned it on one of their guys who left town in a hurry."

Before she got in the front seat Mrs. Bell gave me a hug and said, *"Good luck Danny. If you see your roommate, be sure to thank him for the tee shirt."*

After they drove off I walked across the street to say goodbye to Veronica and when I saw her struggling to get her suitcase down the stairs I rushed up to give her a hand.

"Thank you" she said. *"I had things under control, but I appreciate the help."*

After we put the suitcase into her car she turned and gave me a long hug.

"Well, I guess this is goodbye", she said sadly.

"Let's not say goodbye. How about, see you later? Even if we don't ever see each other again I need something to look forward to. And when you see Michael tell him there are no hard feelings. I know it was an accident. He was too drunk to kick me in the face intentionally."

After she kissed me on the cheek, she gave me a postcard with a picture of the camp club log cabin and a stamp addressed to her at college.

"Let me know how things are going at college. Freshman year can be pretty rough. You're going to be homesick. But you'll get over it. Maybe I'll visit you. If you invite me."

After I promised to write, we both noticed an unusual-looking man who was watching us from a bench across the street. He was wearing a white linen suit, a wide brim fedora hat and dark aviator sunglasses. Next to him were two large suitcases.

"Danny, do you recognize that person?" Veronica asked. *"I think he's been watching us. He looks out of place. Do you want me to call security?"*

"No" I said. *"I'll talk to him, ask a few questions. See what he is doing here. If he seems the least bit dangerous, I'll tap my leg. Then you should call security."*

It wasn't that I was feeling particularly brave that day, or trying to impress Veronica, I just felt numb from everything that had gone on and wanted the drama to be over. I had no idea who the individual on the bench was. He could have been anybody or nobody.

However, as I walked cautiously across the street toward him I noticed something vaguely familiar about the way his right leg was thrown over his left leg and as I got closer I saw that he hadn't actually been watching us at all. He was reading a book. In fact, I wasn't even sure he had noticed us across the street packing up Veronica's car. As I approached, he pulled a slip of paper from inside the brim of his fedora hat and slipped it into the book to mark his place. Then he stood up and said *"I was wondering when you would notice me."*

When I didn't recognize the handsome, clean shaven man standing before me he took off his hat I finally saw that it was Julian. Without a beard he looked completely different.

"I didn't want to interrupt your goodbyes" he said, as he removed his sunglasses.

"I got a job teaching Eastern Religions at NYU: Buddhism, Hinduism and Confucianism. I'm catching the bus and staying with friends in Chelsea until I find my own place. Here's the address, just in case you ever find yourself in lower Manhattan. Don't be a Stranger.

"Speaking of strange, did you know a Greyhound bus stops right here in front of Camp Club twice a week and goes all the way to midtown Manhattan? I didn't. I mean, how could we miss that? It's like a metaphor, if we fail to notice something as large as a Greyhound bus that comes in and out of our lives twice a week for an entire summer, what else are we missing? What I'm saying man, is everything is right in front of us, if we take the time to look around. It's easy to get caught up with the little things in life, the noise and the confusion, and miss

the big picture. The buses that are constantly coming and going when we're not present. Whatever happens in your life, try to remember you're never stuck. You are just not noticing the busses that are continually pulling up to the curb and opening their doors for us to get onboard."

A film director could not have planned it any better because as soon as Julian finished talking, a Greyhound bus pulled up in front of the bench where we were sitting and took him away. Unfortunately, that was the last I ever saw of him and I often wondered if he ever settled down and eventually got married and had a family. Whatever became of him, and whatever he did with the rest of his life, I was certain it was interesting and not what anyone expected.

After Veronica left, I walked back up to the Inn and waited in the lobby for my mother to pick me up. Mrs. Burdler was nowhere to be found and had posted a new sign promoting her "*Fall Foliage Tours*". I was glad she wasn't around because I'm not sure what would have come out of my mouth if I had seen her. After I bought myself a few postcards from the gift shop, my mother pulled up in front of the Inn and jumped out of the car to give me a hug.

"There he is!" my mother shouted as she ran towards me. *"I missed you so much"*

I did my best to listen attentively as she rambled on excitedly about what had been going on back home that summer, but my mind was busy replaying a highlight reel of what had happened that summer as we drove past Camp Club, the swimming pool and the golf course for the last time. When we drove underneath the sign that spelled out *"Welcome to Buck Hill Falls"* in white birch tree branches, I asked her if she wouldn't mind if I listening to my Walkman on the way home and after she said that was okay, I plunked in the cassette *Bridge over Troubled Water* and played *"Homeward Bound"* by Simon and Garfunkel.

I'm sitting in the railway station
Got a ticket to my destination
On a tour of one-night stands
My suitcase and guitar in hand
And every stop is neatly planned
For a poet and a one-man band

Homeward bound

I wish I was

Homeward bound

Home where my thought's escaping

Home where my music's playing

Home where my love lies waiting

Silently for me

It was strange waking up in my childhood bedroom the next morning after being away for the entire summer and in some ways it felt like everything that had happened had all been a dream. My mother wanted to hear all about Veronica, and she made a face when I told her she already had a boyfriend, but forgot to tell me about him. I left out the part about the fight and Julian shacking up with Mrs. Bell and only touched on what had happened with the corrupt General Manager, because she mentioned she had seen an article in the *Allentown Morning Call*. Finally, she asked me if we were going to get the money that Bob had promised from the estate settlement and I told her probably not.

"Things got complicated. Bob Robertson introduced me to dad's first wife and she hired some lawyers to make it look like I did some things that I didn't do. That way, she would get all the money. And I said some things I probably should not have said. So I wouldn't count on us getting anything. I guess I messed up. I'm sorry Mom. But we will figure something out."

Heavy raindrops pelted against my bedroom window that night but the next day was beautiful, and the leaves were just starting to turn color, so my mom made sandwiches and we brought them to a playground around the corner from our house where I had gone to nursery school and ate our lunches at a picnic table. All around us were children playing. A mother who looked a little like a younger version of my mother was pushing her son on a swing and he squealed with laughter as he begged her to push him higher and higher.

"I remember when you were that age" she told me. *"I hoped it would never end. Life is simple through the eyes of a child. Feed them. Play with them. Love them. Push them on a swing and they're happy. It's too bad we outgrow that. Life is simple. I'm not sure why, but the older we get, the more we make everything so damn complicated."*

"When your father and I first met things were pretty simple. I was working as a waitress at a fancy hotel in Philadelphia. I needed the money and it was a job. Your dad was staying at the hotel and had just finished a meeting with a lawyer that didn't go well. He said he was in the middle of a bitter divorce. We talked about how we both needed a break and he told me he had always wanted to visit Annapolis. We kidded about going together and at one point he turned and said 'Let's do it. Let's go. You're not married and I'm separated. We're both miserable. No strings attached. I promise to be a perfect gentleman. Separate bedrooms, if you want. As long as you love fresh seafood and shallow conversation, we are guaranteed to have a good time."

"I was a pretty good judge of character back then, and I trusted him. It was a part time job and I had only two days left so I quit early and we drove to Annapolis where we watched the sun come up and had breakfast at a marina where he rented a sailboat. He was a good sailor."

"For two days we sailed around the Chesapeake Bay, ate seafood and laughed until our sides ached. He had a wonderful smile, just like you. We got together a few more times after that and the following year God gave us you. Your dad was overjoyed

when I told him I was pregnant. We planned a small wedding in Annapolis as soon as his divorce was finalized.

Three weeks before the wedding, he said he had to go to the Bahamas for a business meeting. He promised me he'd be back just as soon as the meeting was over. I drove him to the airport, we said goodbye and that was the last I ever heard from him. Bob told me something happened to him during the business trip, but that didn't make sense. Your dad was so smart, so cautious. The only thing that made any sense was that he left us, intentionally. I blamed myself for whatever made him run away and hide. It wasn't you, he wanted to have kids, it was me."

All of a sudden she broke down and the tears she had had been holding back all those years began to flow uncontrollably down the sides of her cheeks.

"Then, two or three years later, I got a call from one of his professors at Princeton. He told me your father had been asked by the State Department to help them investigate a company he had invested in. They had found out it was actually a front for a gun running operation in Angola. He didn't want any part of it, but he couldn't sell it to someone else knowing what they actually did. As Bob told you, your father was a very ethical man. So he

agreed to meet with the owners in the Bahamas at a place called Graycliff and wear a microphone. But his partner sold him out and he either went into hiding or was killed. We don't know for sure, we might never know. But what's important is that you know your father was a good person. He was brave and he was loyal to his friends and he did his best not to let people down. It breaks my heart that you never got to know each other, because he would have been very proud of you."

The following morning, several hours before my 5:45 AM wakeup call the '66 Galaxie ragtop with one cockeyed headlight rattled across a darkened trestle bridge that spanned the banks of the Lehigh river. In the background loomed the gigantic rusting carcass of Bethlehem Steel. Making his rounds that morning, Floyd "The Hitman" Hardapple, who had represented New York in the finals of the *Golden Gloves* at *Madison Square Garden* in 1954, reached down into the shifting sea of neatly rolled newspapers and expertly tossed the *Allentown Morning Call* out the driver side window. After hearing stories about gang activity in the neighborhood, he started keeping the *Sig Sauer* on the seat next to him under the newspapers for easy access. Even if he never ran into trouble, it felt comfortable to have a friend nearby. The headline that morning proclaimed, *"Military coup in the Congo. Corrupt government crumbles"*

Across town, another car raced across the same trestle bridge at a high rate of speed loosening several rivets in the rusting steel plates. It was impossible to see who was behind the wheel, but Frank Sinatra was belting out *"Summer Wind"* on the radio.

> *The summer wind came blowin' in from across the sea*
> *It lingered there, to touch your hair and walk with me*

The unidentified car accelerated as it approached a four way intersection and the brake lights never came on as it blasted through a red light causing a group of startled pigeons to flee for their lives. When the speeding car approached Floyd's Galaxie, and pulled up directly behind him, he thought about reaching for the handgun, but for some reason he didn't. Instincts told him to wait to see if anyone got out of the car. After a few tense moments he saw the turn signal go on and the car pulled around him and sped away.

All summer long we sang a song and then we
strolled that golden sand
Two sweethearts and the summer wind

The speeding car slowed down when it came to my high school which was around the time my alarm clock went off awakening me at 5:45 AM. Downstairs I smelled toast and I could hear my mother making a fresh pot of coffee.

The autumn wind, and the winter winds they
have come and gone
And still the days, those lonely days, they go on
and on

While I was getting dressed, my mother poured two cups of coffee into mugs and set them down on the breakfast table next to some buttered toast. As she was waiting for me to come downstairs, she walked around the house looking at the life she had created for the two of us. Opening the door to the pantry closet she ran her fingers over the pencil marks she had made when she measured my height on every birthday.

And guess who sighs his lullabies through nights

that never end?

My fickle friend, the summer wind

On her desk my mother picked up a pencil holder I made in school out of a soup can and colored sheets of construction paper cut into the shapes of dinosaurs. Next to the pencil holder was a picture of me proudly holding out a fish I had caught with my grandfather on the first day of Spring. Glancing up from the picture of me as an eight year old, my mother saw me standing at the foot of the stairs ten years later about to go off to college.

The summer wind

Warm summer wind

The summer wind

"*Wow, that was fast.*" she said. "*What can I get you for breakfast?*"

"*Nothing*" I told her. "*I'm ready to go. He should be here any minute.*"

"*Danny, take a bite of toast. Make me feel like I've been a good mother.*"

"You have been a good mother. You've given me everything I need."

"I'm going to miss you so much" she told me, wiping a tear from her eye.

"I know. I'm going to miss you too. But I'll be back for Thanksgiving."

At the end of our street the speeding car slowed down to crawl as the driver appeared to be looking at the house numbers before taking a sharp left turn into our driveway. As soon as we saw the car waiting in the driveway, I picked up my duffle bag and pillow and after my mom locked the side door, we walked over to the car, but before we could reach for the handle , Bob Robertson got out and offered to help my mother with her small suitcase.

"Thanks for getting up so early Bob" my mother says as she handed him her bag.

"The pleasure is all mine. Thank you for allowing me to accompany you to Williamsburg. I always looked forward to dropping a child off at college and this might be my only chance."

"Don't thank me Bob. It was Danny's idea. I'm glad you two found each other. One thing I've learned is, whenever two lost souls find each other, things have a way of working out."

THE END